DIE TO A DISTANT DRUM

Also by William Arden

THE GOLIATH SCHEME

DEAL IN VIOLENCE

A DARK POWER

DIE TO
A DISTANT DRUM

by William Arden

A Red Badge Novel of Suspense

DODD, MEAD & COMPANY · NEW YORK

Copyright © 1972 by William Arden
All rights reserved
No part of this book may be reproduced in any form
without permission in writing from the publisher

ISBN: 0-396-06491-4
Library of Congress Catalog Card Number: 78-180926
Printed in the United States of America
by Vail-Ballou Press, Inc., Binghamton, N.Y.

*To Leo and Cylvia Margulies,
for old times*

Part One

Part One

1

Gilmore, California, is a railroad-junction city east of Los Angeles named for some long-forgotten superintendent of the Union Pacific Railroad. Until recently, the town was almost as forgotten as the superintendent, existed only for the railroad and its yards. But that made land cheap, and in the last few years light industry has begun to move in to build small plants and warehouses along the shabbier streets at the edge of the city. In a time when small business must compete with giants, these little factories tend to change hands rapidly.

On this night in September, the one small plant and two warehouses on an outer street of rooming houses were all shut and silent. An unusually hot night for the time of year, a stifling *santana* wind blowing down the empty street.

Kane Jackson, at a window of a darkened room in the rooming house across the night street from the single plant, didn't notice either the wind or the heat. The tall industrial agent watched a pale green Cadillac turn into the dirt alley at the side of the rooming house. His thin mouth and strong jaw were set in a scowl under his heavy tan. His close-set brown eyes watched a big, well-dressed, middle-aged man come out of the alley and turn into the rooming house. Jackson's large nose twitched once, and that was all.

Slim and muscular, his gray-brown hair bleached in streaks by the California sun, he wore an old, stained pair of army fatigues, and stood there at the window without moving after the well-dressed man had entered his rooming house. His eyes studied the dark street for signs of anyone else until the quick knock came on his room door. He took a long, thin, Mexican cigar from his fatigue pocket, lit it, and smoked in silence.

The knocking came again.

Jackson smoked.

After a few more minutes the door opened and the well-dressed driver of the Cadillac came into the room. The man stood in the open doorway, watched Kane Jackson.

"Close the door," Jackson said. He went on watching the night street below. "I told you to stay away from me, Callison."

The big man, Edgar Callison, closed the door. "It's been two weeks. You didn't call. I've got a right to expect results. For a thousand dollars a day, I've got rights."

Callison was a big-faced man of fifty, pale and soft in his pulpy features. His blue eyes were so light they seemed to disappear in the dark room, leaving only shining holes in his face. He wore an expensive gray suit, rich black shoes, a black homburg, and a dark blue striped tie. A diamond caught stray light on his left hand, and his wet mouth was nervous.

"I guaranteed a maximum fee. Time is my problem," Jackson said, turning to the big man. "I work my way or not at all."

Callison wiped sweat from his heavy face, sat down. "I don't have your nerves. Spying is new to me."

"It's not to me," Jackson said, smoked his thin cigar. "Waiting is ninety percent of the game. You shouldn't get into things you can't handle. You broke my rules, I could call it off and keep the money."

"All right, I'm sorry," Callison said, sweated, "but why is it taking so long? I hired you because you're supposed to be the best in the whole dirty business. The top man."

"I am," Jackson said, turned back to look out the window again. "It's taking time because I am the best spy in the trade. This is a tricky job, Callison—if you want your information without John Marker knowing that you got it—ever."

Jackson seemed to contemplate the small, narrow, two-story, yellow brick industrial plant across the dark street from the rooming house. A sign over a padlocked steel grating at the main entrance read: Marker Industrial Chemical Co. There was no sign of light or activity in the building. A wider avenue bordered one side, and a deserted parking lot the other.

"The plant's on complete stand-by, no production going on," Jackson said. "No workers, no office staff, no tooling-up crew, not even maintenance crews. Only John Marker himself, a secretary, and a night watchman. The equipment is inside, but it's not even hooked up for power. There's nothing to cover me, Callison. No matter what excuse I tried to use to get in, I'd stand out like a sore thumb, and the moment you acted on the information I got, Marker would remember me and know what happened. In a plant where nothing is happening, there's not much I could use for a cover story, and whatever I tried to say I was could be blown in an instant. When you hired me, I guaranteed no suspicion of espionage."

Callison wiped at his face. "Then can't you break in? An expert like you shouldn't leave any evidence."

Jackson shook his head. "The people who built that plant in the first place put in a vault I couldn't crack inside of four hours, and not without leaving evidence—unless I can get inside twice in the same night, and have six hours to sit and wait undisturbed. You understand?"

"What I understand," Callison said, "is that you sound like a man weaseling out! If it's that hard, how do you ever expect to get what I want?"

Jackson went on watching the street below, smoking his cigar, not looking at Callison. "I've already gotten most of it. Your confidential list of sales prospects for the new adhesive—Marker has it all right. Your cost analysis figures, he has them, too. The raw material costs. He took it all with him when he quit you, I've got copies to prove it."

"The damned thief!" Callison swore. "I'll hang him! What about the full research data on the new process for the adhesive? He can't get anywhere without that, he doesn't have the whole thing in his own head."

"Tonight," Jackson said, looked at his watch. "I'll know about that, and everything else of yours he might have taken with him, in three hours now. Does that suit you?"

In the chair where he sat, Callison bit his fingernails. His whole, heavy body seemed to tremble with an eagerness, but there was doubt in his almost invisible eyes.

"If it was so hard, how did you do it? You're sure there won't be any trace? I can't risk—"

"Come here," Jackson said.

He was alert now, looking down into the dark street. Callison joined him at the window. Jackson nodded down toward a panel truck parked half a block up the street from the Marker Chemical plant. Four people had gotten out of the truck—two men and two women. They all carried something, and walked quickly to the side entrance to the Marker Chemical plant, looking all around them as they hurried. A brief, faint light showed at the side door. Another man appeared from inside, unlocked the steel grille that protected the side entrance, and all five vanished inside. It all happened in seconds, the dark street silent and empty again.

Kane Jackson said, "The night watchman is John Marker's son, Adam. He stays there all night, alone. For the last three weeks he's been letting those four inside to use the plant's labs, equipment, and chemicals. They stay in there working all night, no one knows they exist."

"Working? On what?" Callison said, stared at the plant.

"On bombs," Jackson said. "They're underground terrorists, Callison—Weathermen. Revolutionaries, home-grown variety, and Adam Marker is one of them. The five of them are a secret Weatherman group. Only now there are six members."

"Six?"

"Me," Jackson said. He turned from the window now, dropped his cigar into an ashtray. "It took me almost the two weeks I've worked for you to arrange it. That's what you pay me for—my knowledge, experience, and contacts. I know more about some bombs and fuses than almost anyone outside the army, and I've got the contacts to make me a believable member of Weatherman."

"What contacts? Revolutionaries? Underground terrorism?"

"In military espionage, Callison, a man plays a lot of roles, meets a lot of people, learns a lot of secrets. Three days ago I joined the group over there as a professional fuse expert sent down from their brothers in Seattle as go-betweens. They need me, I can play the role, and it's let me move around inside the plant at will with no one to bother me, and no one who'll ever say I was there."

Callison sweated again. "But, when they find out that you're not really one of them, then they'll—"

"They won't find out. What do you think took me two weeks of preparation? No matter how far they look into my fake Weatherman record, they'll find an old militant. But they won't look, they won't care as long as their attack goes off smoothly, and they'll never spot me later by accident."

"Damn it, what will they do when your fuses don't work, Jackson? When the bombs don't go off? They'll know a fake—"

"No fake, Callison," Jackson said. He began to pull on a pair of thin black gloves. "My fuses will work, the bombs will go off."

Callison stared at Jackson. "You'll really . . . ? Where? What are they going to blow up? What if someone—?"

"What they blow up isn't my business," Jackson said. He took a small, 7.65-mm Mauser automatic from under his fatigues, checked it, put it back.

Collison started to say something more, thought better of it, looked out the window and across at the dark chemical plant.

"Now get out of here," Jackson said. "And don't be seen, or all bets are off."

The industrial spy remained silent at the window after Callison had gone. He watched the heavy man turn into the alley, waited until the Cadillac backed out and drove away. He saw no one and nothing on the street. As far as he could tell, no one had seen Callison come or go. He swore silently at the businessman anyway, before he picked up a small, black bag and went out.

2

A slender youth opened the side door of the plant, unlocked the gate for Jackson.

"You're late. Walton's pretty mad."

"Walton likes to be mad, Marker," Jackson said, followed the youth into the building and along a dark gray corridor.

"He's got reasons," Adam Marker said.

The youth was short, with a large nose and soft, vulnerable brown eyes. His hair was dark, worn medium long, and he walked slowly, almost reluctantly, as if he didn't really want to move his legs at all, as if there was nowhere he wanted to go. When he reached the end of the dark corridor he opened a heavy fire door, and the two men entered a large laboratory of benches, fume hoods, and rows of bottles stacked on metal shelves.

A tall, square-faced, red-headed man in his thirties paced just inside the door. He wore gray work pants, heavy boots, and a Marine Corp sweatshirt. His angry face was scarred with a bullet-wound scar, and both his hands were welted with the scars of shrapnel wounds.

"You're late again, Jackson," the tall man said.

"Report me to someone," Jackson said dryly.

"We don't report, we eliminate! You know our rules. This is a disciplined group, or it's nothing. You follow the rules here, or you get out!"

Jackson set down his small bag, lit one of his thin cigars. He smoked and watched the tall man. "Rules are good, Walton, so is discipline. But you've got to know what rules, and when to apply discipline. I was working undercover while you were still playing marbles. I work to my own discipline. I was here, working, hours ago tonight. If you don't like my work, then tell me to get out."

At a long lab bench farther into the big room, an older man had been listening. In his fifties, stocky, he had the battered face of old tramps on any skid row, and the bright, fanatic eyes of a man who had spent his life making great plans. His whole manner as he worked with wires and an electric soldering iron, was alert and cautious. Now he spoke to Walton:

"We need his work, Frank. He knows his job."

Frank Walton turned on the older man. "Brunner, you let me handle—!"

Walton stopped. The two women working at the same bench as the older man, Brunner, looked up to watch Frank Walton. The red-headed militant took a slow breath, turned back to Jackson. His tense face relaxed a little— but only a little. The face eased, not the gray eyes that seemed embedded like stones in his face. Eyes that didn't seem to be part of the rest of Walton, that watched himself as coldly as they watched everyone else. They watched Jackson now.

"All right, we need you, Jackson. Maybe I'm too rigid, but that's what I learned a man has to be. I care for nothing and no one who doesn't think, act, exactly as I do. I had my last compromise, my last friendly smile, burned out of me in those two years in the Pendleton brig. I squeezed out the last trace of middle-class values, habits, ideals. All I care about is to destroy this society."

The scarred ex-Marine sat against a lab bench, his eyes fixed only on Jackson. "You and Brunner are old rebels, yes, experienced, but sometimes that worries me. You old left types have failed too often, you're willing to settle for too little. We're revolutionists, not reformers. We don't want to scare the rulers here into giving us something, some change, we want to destroy them, destroy this world so we can build a new world based on human values not money values. Sometimes I'm not sure you old rebels have the ruthlessness to do it."

While Frank Walton talked, the two women had gone back to their work. Adam Marker had joined them, was bent busily over a delicate clock mechanism. Only the older man, Brunner, wasn't working.

"We've learned to control our rage, Frank," Brunner said.

"Too much control is cowardice," Frank Walton said. "Too much patience means doing nothing."

"Then maybe we better do something," Jackson said.

"All right, we'll work. You have the new fuses?"

"Yes."

"You want to work here with the explosives?"

Walton nodded around the big laboratory. An unused lab—not abandoned, but not yet put into operation. The fume hoods were unconnected, the lab benches were bare except where the group was working, the water in the sinks wasn't turned on. Only the bench where the two women, Adam Marker, and the older man named Brunner worked, was in use. This bench was piled with electronic parts, sticks of dynamite, and blocks of plastic explosive. Army manuals were open on the bench.

"No, too risky," Jackson said. "I set up in the small lab down the corridor when I was here earlier. I don't much like fusing with amateurs and dynamite around."

The taller and older of the two women laid down her dynamite. "Are you afraid to die, Mr. Jackson? Or do you just distrust amateurs, especially women?"

She was tall and thin, with blond hair worn long. A woman of twenty-six or so, she had a narrow, aristocratic face, and full, heavy breasts unusual for her thin body. Her denim shirt and stained jeans were tailored on her good, slim body, as if she had worn custom-made clothes all her life and couldn't escape the habit even now. One of the children of privilege and affluence turned revolutionary, and her patrician face had the fierce asceticism of a medieval monk.

"I think women can do anything they want, Miss Blake, and sometimes they make better fighters than men. I don't like amateurs, men or women," Jackson said. "And do you particularly want to die?"

There was a sneer in her eyes. "It's not very important if any of us live or die, is it? Only the end counts."

"That's the mistake of an amateur, Miss Blake," Jackson said. "Right, Brunner?"

The older man, Brunner, nodded. "It's our job to stay alive if we can, Amanda. Work, fight, destroy the past as long as we can, as much as we can. A trained revolutionary is hard to replace, Jackson is right. No one has replaced Guevara yet, he made a bad mistake."

"You'd rather give up a mission than die trying?" Amanda Blake said hotly.

"Alive, we can succeed another day," Brunner snapped. "Dead we can accomplish nothing."

"I think you're a coward, Emil," the tall girl said. "No guts at all, and no real revolutionary!"

"And I think you're an arrogant, overprivileged amateur!" Emil Brunner said. "You want to outrevolution the blacks, outdare Guevara, and be more male than any man. In the end your self-image is more important than the movement, the group, or any single mission. You'll ruin us all, Amanda."

The girl was up. "If you think that—!"

"Hold it!" Frank Walton stood at the tall girl's side, his arm around her shoulders. He glared at Emil Brunner. "You lay off Amanda, Emil, you hear? You're not boss here, no one is! You've got the experience, and we need it, but in guts Amanda's worth ten of you. Don't judge her or anyone."

Walton held the tall girl close to him. She reached up, held his arm. Together they watched the others, a pair. Emil Brunner looked at them, shrugged, and sat down again at the long lab bench, picked up his soldering iron. Adam Marker seemed to study his own hands that held a block of plastic explosive. The second woman, the only one of the group who had said nothing since Jackson had come in, looked at Brunner.

"Dad?" she said. "We've got to work together until after the refinery, don't we? We can't fight now. Amanda's too superior sometimes, but you shouldn't have said she'll ruin us. Frank's right."

She smiled at Frank Walton. She was a small, dark girl no more than twenty, and her eyes were large and soft as she smiled at Walton. Shy eyes, and yet eager. Jackson sensed at once that she was more than a little interested in Frank Walton. As she picked up her tools to go back to her work, her small hands shook, and her face was flushed.

"We need each other, all of us," she said.

"Rosa's right," Frank Walton said. "Nothing matters but blowing that refinery tomorrow. No personalities, okay?"

"No woman-chasing, either?" Adam Marker said.

"Adam you keep—!" Frank Walton began.

Amanda Blake stood up at the bench. "I have to leave for an hour. I'll be back before we start rehearsing."

The tall girl walked into the corridor. Jackson felt the tensions and antagonisms of the group hanging in the silent laboratory. The troubles inside a small group that had to surface from the enforced closeness, the danger of their work, the raw nerves as the time for action drew closer. But Jackson had no interest in the clashes of the group. What they did or didn't do wasn't his worry now. He had his own work to do. He made his voice calm, soothing, businesslike.

"Let's all listen to Miss Brunner. You need my fuses tonight, and you have to rehearse the attack. I'll work in the small lab, and everyone stay away until I finish. That understood?"

"Yes," Frank Walton said. "We'll be ready when you have the fuses. Okay, let's get some work done."

Jackson picked up his small bag, walked out into the corridor.

3

Inside the smaller lab at the other end of the gray corridor, Jackson locked the door and listened. There were no sounds in the corridor. No one had followed him from the big laboratory.

He went to a lab table where he had laid out his caps, timers, wires and connections earlier that night—at precisely 6:05 P.M. to be exact. He opened his small suitcase, took out a set of detailed drawings, looked at his watch, and went to work on the fuse assemblies. He worked steadily, neither nervous nor hurrying.

Two hours later he sat back, looked at his watch again, and lit a cigar. He smoked in silence, not moving, his eyes half closed. When the cigar was almost gone, he looked once more at his watch. It was just ten minutes before midnight. He disconnected two simple points on his fuse assemblies, picked up his black bag, and went to the other door of the lab opposite the corridor door.

He opened the door with a key on his ring of special keys, slipped out into a narrow fire stairs, and went up to the second floor. He listened for a moment before stepping out into the dark, carpeted corridor of the office section of the plant. He walked past glassed office doors, all empty and without names, to the last door in the corridor marked: John Marker, President. He used his keys again.

Inside the office, he crossed the outer area with its secretarial desk, used his keys for a third time, and stood in the plush office of John Marker. He paid no attention to the desk or files, he had been through them the night before. Instead, he went to a closet, opened it, and squatted down in front of an innocent-looking little box disguised as a telephone connection. Delicately, like a jeweler at work, he unscrewed the cover of the box, and surveyed the miniaturized mechanism inside. It was a relay alarm system, set to go off in the remote station of a central security company, and bring the security company guards on the run.

Jackson opened his small bag, took out a compact instrument with connecting wires coming out of each end. He carefully connected both wires of the electronic bypass switch to the contacts on each side of the alarm trip. He stood up, took his bag, and closed the closet door. When the vault opened now, no contacts would be broken to trigger the alarm. He went to the plush desk of John Marker, sat down, lit one of his thin cigars.

His tanned face quiet and immobile, he smoked and listened to the night. In his military years Jackson had learned what every spy alone in an enemy city learns—that there is no silence that is ever really silent. Everything on earth, the earth itself, is alive and moving if we are quiet enough, alert enough, to hear. Now the building itself made small sounds. Hidden beams creaked, perhaps from faint earth tremors in this region of earthquakes where the land was never at rest. A stray car passed on the avenue outside, rare this late at night on the outer streets of Gilmore. The steady rumble of diesels and clank of box cars carried from the railroad yards.

Over all the night sounds Jackson heard, the faint click was like a gunshot. A click that came from the massive vault in the left wall. Jackson pinched out his cigar and put it into his pocket. He wiped the ashtray with a soft rag he carried, brushed the seat of the desk chair, checked the desk carefully with his eyes, picked up his bag again, and went to the vault.

At the vault he attached a wire to the time-lock wheel, plugged the wire into a wall socket, and removed a thick sleeve from the hub of the lock wheel—the magnetic sleeve demagnetized by the current from the wall socket. He gently placed the sleeve-instrument into its case in his bag —it had done its job. Set on the time-lock wheel at exactly 6 P.M. that night, its delicate electronic mechanism had doubled the speed of the time lock to make it open in exactly half its set time.

He took a microscope glass and examined the time-lock wheel to be sure that his electronic sleeve had left no scratches. It hadn't. From his back he picked out a large, flat disk with felt-lined chuck jaws on one side, and a black-and-white wheel dial on the other. He set the chuck jaws carefully on the knob of the combination lock, tightened them down, and began to turn the large disk clockwise.

After a few moments, the wheel dial on the flat disk flipped over from white on top to black on top. Jackson noted the combination setting, continued to turn the large disk clockwise. It turned all the way back to where Jackson had started the circle with nothing more happening. Jackson spun the big disk to reset the combination.

Once more he turned the large disk to where the wheel dial had flipped over the first time. It flipped again. This time Jackson turned his large disk back counterclockwise until the wheel dial flipped black-up once more. He noted this dial setting of the combination, and continued the same careful process, noting each time the wheel dial flipped over on the faint electronic signal set up in the large disk by a tumbler falling in the combination lock, until he had the combination and opened the outer vault door.

He removed the large disk instrument, checked with his microscope glass for any scratches on the combination knob, and replaced the disk in his bag. Then he unlocked the inner vault door with a key on his ring of keys, and went into the vault.

Methodically, working from left to right, he examined the contents of each drawer in the vault. After half an hour he had three documents laid out on the floor, the last drawer examined and closed. One of the documents was a file of six sheets, the other two were single sheets. He pressed each document sheet, one at a time, against a sheet of sensitized paper.

When he had copied each page from the vault documents, he slipped the copies into a black envelope, and inserted the envelope into a hidden compartment in his small bag. He replaced each document in the drawer he had taken it from, in the exact place, and wiped each drawer with his gloved hands. He closed the inner vault door, relocked it with his key. He reset the time lock for the morning, closed the outer vault door, spun the combination, and examined the whole door once again for any scratches.

In the silent office he stood out in the center and turned in a slow circle, seeing every inch of the room the way it had been when he first entered, his mind as sure of the way the office had been as if he had taken a photograph. He didn't hurry. All his senses concentrated to be sure that he would leave no trace of his presence—but not quite one-hundred percent of all his senses.

Over a lifetime of working where every motion, every sound, every smell, could be the signal of instant danger, his senses were always at work like antennae in all directions—constant and ceaseless, aware of every slight signal no matter how small, dangerous or innocent. It was one of the many things that had driven his ex-wife, Cassie, to leave him. ("I can't stand it, Kane. You never see, or hear, or smell anything without coming alert, analyzing it. Even in bed! I can't breathe that way!")

This time it was a sound—soft and light.

The sound of someone stepping lightly out in the carpeted corridor. Or something. A noise of the building? A small animal? A rat in the empty building? A cat? Or someone?

Motionless, nothing changed on Jackson's face where he stood in the office. Outwardly, no one could have seen the slightest change in him. Inwardly, his brain changed its whole focus, his muscles shifted to the new command, ready to glide him into cover, ready to reach in a second for his Mauser.

He stood that way for two minutes—an eternity when a man listens and waits.

The sound did not come again.

Jackson waited another full minute.

Silence.

His brain shifted again, his eyes continued their check of the office from where they had stopped at the sound. The danger gone, his mind forgot it at once. For a spy, apprehension can't exist. The instant danger seems gone it must be forgotten. Only real, immediate danger can be a cause for alarm if a spy, any kind of spy, is to do his work and remain sane.

So his eyes went on with their check of the office, the alarm of the sound in the corridor wiped away unless, and until, it came again. There was no evidence in the office of his work. He left, locked all doors behind him, and went down to the first floor to reconnect his fuse assemblies.

The five Weathermen all looked up as Jackson came into the large laboratory.

"Okay, the fuses are ready," he said.

He studied them all for any sign of suspicion of him, any change in their manner toward him, anything to show that one of them could have been in the corridor upstairs to see or hear him in John Marker's office. He saw nothing.

The red-headed ex-Marine, Frank Walton, and Amanda Blake, got up and left the laboratory to get the fuses. Adam Marker sat back from his work, his thin face tight as if the readiness of Jackson's fuses had made him realize that they were actually going to explode real bombs. Rosa Brunner went on working, her young face sweating, her childish hands shaking on the dynamite. Emil Brunner stood up.

"How close can your fuses be timed?" Brunner asked.

"Theoretically, within two seconds, but I don't advise cutting it that close," Jackson said. "Too much human error and chance involved. If you slipped, you'd go up with the bomb."

Brunner nodded. "We don't want to lose anyone, but we have to time it to go off as soon as we're gone. We don't want someone stumbling over it and getting killed. We don't want people hurt by our bombs at this stage."

"The public wouldn't like that," Jackson said.

"No, not now. Later, it may be useful to assassinate government and industry leaders, the real war criminals."

"Not until you can convince the people that they *are* war criminals and enemies, break the ideological hold the leaders have on the majority," Jackson said. "If you can do that. It's not so easy to convince people that they believe what they do because they've been fooled, duped."

"It never has been," Emil Brunner said. "But we'll do it, as long as we let nothing stand in our way."

Before Jackson could answer the old revolutionary, Frank Walton and the tall Blake woman returned, each with a tray of Jackson's assembled fuses. They carried them carefully, set them down on the long lab bench, but they didn't sweat or shake. Their eyes were bright with what Jackson guessed was a feeling of power, of strength, the deadly fuses gave them.

Adam Marker stood up and walked to the trays. With Emil Brunner and the other two, the thin youth looked down at the fuses. He reached and touched them, almost gently.

"Beautiful, aren't they?" Amanda Blake said, her ascetic face glowing, her hand holding Frank Walton's arm, squeezing.

"Let's get them ready now," Frank Walton said, the ex-Marine's big, scarred hands opening and closing like an athlete anxious to begin the action.

"No," Emil Brunner said. "We won't fuse the bombs until just before we go tomorrow."

"Brunner?" Jackson said. "Look at your daughter."

Rosa Brunner had not left her seat on the long lab bench to look at the fuses. She sat still working to tie sticks of dynamite into a bundle. Her hands were trembling violently, and her pretty young face was beaded with sweat. It was hot in the lab, but not that hot. She jumped at the sound of Jackson's voice talking about her, dropped the dynamite. Her hands held hard to the edge of the bench, and her chest heaved as if she wasn't aware that dynamite can't explode by being dropped. She looked up, tried to smile, but her eyes were too nervous—and something else. Wide, luminous eyes; wet and dilated.

"She's nervous, not used to this work yet," Emil Brunner said. "Her first mission."

Jackson watched the young girl closely. Rosa Brunner was nervous, yes, and it was hot, yes, but there was something about her eyes. The industrial agent needed some excuse to leave as soon as he could, this could be it. He knew what those eyes, the sweat and the trembling could mean. So did Frank Walton.

"God damn it, Brunner," Walton said, his voice low but harsh. "Is she on drugs? Is she? I swear—"

Adam Marker said, "No! She's okay."

"Is she?" Walton said, stared at the girl, and at Adam Marker. "I won't work with anyone who uses drugs, you hear? No one dependent on anything, psychologically or physically, works in any group I'm with!"

"She's not on anything!" Adam Marker said hotly.

Emil Brunner said, "I hope she's not, it's too dangerous in our work. Rosa?"

Brunner's battered face was solemn, the frozen look of a hunted man on his face, the grim rigidity of a man who has spent his life in the back streets of the world working to destroy that world—a face that now had no other goal, no other love, no other duty. He had been underground for a long time, in a lot of places. He knew the necessities of the slow, dangerous, dirty work, and would flinch from nothing necessary. Now he watched his daughter like a judge in some high court.

"I . . . I'm just a little scared, Dad, Frank," Rosa Brunner said. "I . . . took some pills . . . tranquillizers, to calm me down. It's . . . hot. I—"

"Look at her arms, her purse," Frank Walton snapped.

Adam Marker said, "Leave Rosa alone! Don't you touch her."

The thin youth went to the girl, put his hand on her soft shoulder. Rosa Brunner shook his hand off, pushed him away, held her arm out to Frank Walton.

"Look, Frank, go ahead," she said, held out both arms.

Adam Marker walked away into a far corner, his thin back trembling, his hands clenched in fists. Frank Walton held Rosa Brunner's arms. The arms were smooth and unmarked. Rosa's eyes were up toward Frank Walton's face. The ex-Marine dropped her arms, opened her handbag, rummaged in it.

"Nothing," Walton said, dropped the bag on the bench.

"I told you," Rosa Brunner said. "It's just the heat, those pills. I'll be all right."

Jackson said, "Brunner, can you hit the target without her?"

"No, we need everyone," Emil Brunner said.

"Then maybe you should call it off," Jackson said. "We all get out of here now, start again somewhere else."

"She'll be all right," Brunner said.

"We're not calling it off now," Frank Walton said.

Amanda Blake said, "Scared again, Mr. Jackson?"

Jackson had done all he could do without risking them becoming suspicious of him. There was nothing more he could do to stop their plans now. But he had his own cue to leave.

"I'm always scared of trouble, Miss Blake," he said, picked up his black bag. "My job is done here, anyway. I wish you luck, you'll need it from what I've seen around here."

"You don't want to go with us?" Amanda Blake said. "Take Rosa's place if you're so worried about her?"

"I make fuses, not raids. Too old."

He didn't wait for any answer. He left them in silence, Adam Marker in his corner, Rosa Brunner still seated at the long lab bench, and the other three watching him go.

In the rooming house, Jackson closed and locked his room door. He didn't think anyone in the Weatherman group had any suspicions of him or his Weatherman disguise, yet someone could have been in that second floor corridor, and Jackson took no unnecessary chances. He packed his large equipment case, put it with his small black bag ready to take down to his rented car in the alley beside the rooming house, checked the room to be sure he had left no trace, and went to the telephone.

He dialed. The ringing at the other end went on without an answer. He let the phone ring ten times, and hung up. He sat frowning. He didn't check the number, he knew it was the right number—the special contact number where Edgar Callison was supposed to be waiting, reachable at any hour. Aften ten minutes, Jackson dialed the number again. There was still no answer. Jackson hung up, his face thoughtful. Where was . . . ?

The next instant he lay on the floor, his shoulder in pain, his face bleeding where it had hit the edge of a table.

Dazed, he heard the echo of the explosion hammering in his ears, felt the solid shock wave like a heavy blow against him.

Glass of the broken window littered the floor, and the explosion itself seemed to be in the room like time reversed. An explosion outside the rooming house, across the street; two smaller explosions following now, and the acrid odor of dynamite, plastic and fire.

4

Jackson lay on the rooming house floor in the enormous silence that comes after an explosion. A silence like some vast vacuum, as if all the air had been drawn out of the world.

No sound anywhere.

Jackson sat up, felt himself. He was unhurt except for the cut on his face, a bruise on his shoulder. The windows of the room were broken, the telephone, knocked off its cradle, buzzed like a distant wasp, but there was no other damage.

Jackson stood up. He could see the flickering light of flames now, and out on the street frightened, wary voices began to grow audible in the distance up the street. He went to the broken windows.

The Marker Chemical building was a smoking shambles, small flames beginning to rise and flicker over the dark street. The left rear wall had blown out into the parking lot, the rear section of the roof had collapsed. All windows were broken, the roof sagged in the center as if the second floor had partially fallen inside, and the front was leaning but hadn't given way. The parking lot and wide avenue had saved the nearest other buildings from more than minor damage.

All along the dark street, growing suddenly light in the rising flames from the chemical plant, people in night clothes, or half dressed, were coming out of the houses into the street. Most of them just went as far as the sidewalk in front of their houses, and stopped. Jackson didn't look at them. He looked at the Marker Chemical building, what was left of it. Less than two minutes had passed since the explosion, Jackson didn't think anyone could have come out yet—if anyone was coming out.

Jackson had no real connection to the revolutionaries in the shattered plant, no reason to care what had happened to them, and yet . . .

A shadow came out of the smashed front door of the burning building. Shapeless, impossible to tell if it was a man or a woman, the shadow vanished into the night along the avenue.

Moments later, two more figures emerged from a side window, one helping the other, and stumbled up the flickering street to where the pickup truck the group had arrived in was parked. They got in, the truck drove off past the staring residents of the rooming houses gathered on the sidewalk.

Jackson waited. Sirens began to wail far off, both police and fire sirens. Jackson was about to turn from the window when the fourth shape limped from the ruined chemical plant. Alone, the faceless figure crossed the street and disappeared among the rooming houses.

Jackson watched for another minute, the flames high now, licking out of all the shattered windows. No one else came out. Four, that was all. Jackson left the window, and his room, and went down and out into the street.

All along the bright, fire-illuminated street, the tenants of the rooming houses stood in a kind of shocked, yet curious daze. The sirens were closer now, growing louder.

Jackson ran across to the building, began to circle all

around it. The flames were hot and fierce, feeding on the stored chemicals, but Jackson went all around the plant looking for any way inside. There was no way. He searched in the light of the fire for anyone who might have been lying near the building, perhaps injured. There was no one. The sirens were near now, almost at the far end of the street. Some of the residents of the rooming houses moved toward the burning plant, bolder with the imminent approach of knowledge and authority. They would be protected now, and could enjoy the thrill of disaster in safety.

Jackson returned across the street to his rooming house, he wanted no part of the police or the firemen. Now he wanted to leave the area even more urgently before any questions could be asked, his presence there examined. The explosion itself was a stroke of luck now that his job for Edgar Callison was finished.

The bombs were gone and the Weatherman group would scatter now. What they had been doing had to come out once the ruins were searched, the police would be after them. They were finished as a group, and the police would never find them, no. They would vanish into the very real and well-organized underground, and his connection to them would never be known.

Jackson closed the room door, walked quickly to his two suitcases. The police and the fire engines were in the street, he would leave his rented car in the alley and go on foot. The car couldn't be traced to him, a precaution he . . .

The man was hidden in the dim corner of the room away from the windows. A figure, no more, without a face Jackson could see. Jackson reached for his Mauser.

"Slow down, Jackson."

Something glinted in the hand of the man in the corner,

flickering with the light of the flames outside the windows. Jackson let his own hand drop to his side, stood quietly.

"You're alone?" the man said.

Jackson recognized the voice now—Frank Walton. The red-headed ex-Marine stepped out of the corner, limped heavily on his left leg.

"I'm alone," Jackson said. "Is the gun necessary?"

"I had to be sure you were alone," Frank Walton said, sat down in the single armchair in the room, his scarred face wincing once with the pain in his leg. He still held his gun. "Then, I wondered, you know?"

"Wondered?"

"What blew it all?" Walton said. "Brunner's careful, like an old woman. Fuses and bombs separate, material stored at a good distance. How did it blow?"

"You think maybe I did it, somehow?" Jackson said.

"I don't think, I find out," Walton said. "I saw you leave this house after the explosion. Your fuses weren't what blew first. I checked your bags there. A lot of equipment, but no remote radio-trigger I could see."

"None of the fuses or bombs were radio-triggered," Jackson said. "That's lucky for me, isn't it?"

"Lucky," Walton said.

The tall ex-Marine lowered his gun to his lap, leaned his head back, closed his eyes. The light of the flames outside cast shifting light and shadows across his face. Blood and blackened ash on the revolutionary's face. His left trouser leg was torn and burned, blood on the leg and an ugly, swollen wound that showed through the tear. His voice was low, detached, his eyes still closed.

"You have to keep going, you know? Don't let it stop you, get to you." Walton seemed to be talking to the room itself, to something behind his closed eyes—himself, perhaps. A part of himself that had to be talked to, encouraged. "I used to get drunk, smile a lot, worry about people liking me, about women liking me. Out to please, be liked, like everyone else. In the Pendleton brig I was scared at first, I'd tried to buck the Marines, the war over in Nam, and they'd slapped me down hard. I thought for a while maybe I was wrong, no one liked me. I wanted them to rehabilitate me, make me like everyone else, eager and happy."

His eyes still closed, he reached into his breast pocket for a cigarette, winced at the pain in his leg from the small movement. "I found all that eager happiness was the joy of a dog, a pet who wagged his tail when someone gave him a bone and a warm bed. I found out that brigs, prisons, don't rehabilitate rebels, they destroy them. To adapt, be rehabilitated, means psychic destruction, loss of identity, a zero. That's what they want you to be, a zero, and they call it rehabilitation. If you want them to let you live, you have to vanish into the mass like a blob of jelly."

Walton smoked, blew the smoke hard into the liquid light from the burning plant. "I decided I wouldn't let them do that to me. I began to discipline my mind and my body for one thing: revolution. I willed myself to exist, to not care if I lived or died if it meant giving in. I slept four hours a night, studied politics and history in that brig, did pushups all day sometimes to control my sex needs and train my body. I trained out all except my rage at this sick, criminal society, everything except war without terms."

He was silent, then, for a time. The shouts and noises of the firemen all along the street outside, a chaos of machines and voices. Walton opened his eyes. "Accidents happen, you go on. You keep fighting, never let up. Discipline—inside! Where it counts. That's what they don't have, the amateurs and the old, tired revolutionaries. Soft inside, playing a game, still filled with the irrelevant. Personal trivia, personal feelings, individual needs and wants they haven't cleaned out. They haven't purged all the softness of white-skin privilege, the clutter of their minds, so they make mistakes, get careless."

Jackson said, "What went wrong?"

"It blew, that's all."

"What blew? Not my fuses, no," Jackson said.

"I don't know what blew," the ex-Marine said, his gray eyes flat and angry. "We were doing the last stage of the rehearsal, all separated. I was in your small lab, it didn't blow there. I was pinned under a bench. Never saw the others before I got loose and got out."

"Did everyone get out?"

"I don't know. I didn't see any of them. Maybe they're still in there, dead or alive."

"No, three others got out. I think you were last. Who didn't get out?"

"It doesn't matter. I'll know when we regroup, if we do. I'm not sure this group was any good. We'll see. Now I need you, my leg's broken, I think."

He said it in the same voice he had said everything else. His leg was broken, a simple fact to be analyzed and considered as a tactical matter the same as everything else in his life. Cool and rigid, involved only in a war.

"You got here on a broken leg?"

"I had to, but I can't go much farther. You'll contact a man for me—Raymondo Peña. He works at the bookstore at Gilmore City College. He's a Venceremos Brigade man."

"The Cuban travel front?"

"Find him, tell him I'll be at State and South Mojave

at exactly four A.M. Don't be spotted."

"The leg?" Jackson said. He reached for the light switch.

Walton's gun came up. "Don't!"

Jackson took his hand from the light switch.

"Damn it, a light could bring the police. Now get to Peña. Tell him, and come back. If the cops find me first you'll know it. I'll take some of them with me. Every little bit helps."

Jackson turned to pick up his two suitcases.

"Leave those! What's the matter with you, Jackson? What do you think would happen if the cops spotted you in the street carrying those two bags? Don't you know better than that?"

Jackson knew what the police would do if they saw a man near the exploded plant at this hour with two suitcases, and he knew better. It had been a try. He left the bags.

"Stay out of sight, I can be traced to this room, too," Jackson said.

"You won't be through me," Frank Walton said.

Walton closed his eyes again, the pain of his leg on his face. He held his pistol. Jackson went out.

5

The Marker Chemical building still burned, but the firemen had arrived fast, and the fire was already under control. There had been no more explosions, and the emptiness of the shut-down plant had provided less to burn.

Jackson mixed into the crowd of spectators in their pajamas and bathrobes. The police held them back from the fire engines that blocked the street. Thick hoses snaked all across the street, water ran wide in the gutters, engines and motors throbbed and shook, raincoated firemen moved everywhere, their officers shouting orders, hurrying from place to place.

On the edge of the crowd, away from the engines and a little apart, a knot of high-ranking uniformed police and a fire captain was gathered around a short, well-built man in his late forties with a thick, well-groomed head of gray-brown hair. He had a smooth, handsome, strong-jawed face, with a certain arrogance in it, and a vague resemblance to the smaller, softer face of the militant youth, Adam Marker. Jackson recognized the owner of the chemical plant, John Marker, as soon as he saw him among the police. The businessman's face seemed to have collapsed now, like the face of a wax dummy melted by the heat. His eyes were puffed and red in the light of the fire, and he ran one hand through his thick hair over and over like a robot.

Jackson edged closer to the small group, keeping a wary eye on the patrolmen holding back the onlookers. John Marker was talking, his eyes riveted toward the fire that was gutting his building like a caveman who had never seen fire before.

". . . the plunge, right? My own business after twenty years doing all the work and seeing the bosses get the cash," John Marker said, his eyes moving to look at the silent police brass, looking back at the fire, hypnotized. "But that's not it. No. Where is he? Adam? Where's my son?"

"We haven't found any watchman, Mr. Marker," the fire captain said. "I'm sorry. Maybe he got out—"

"Out? Of course he got out! But where is he?" John Marker cried, looked at them, back at the fire. "Maybe he's hurt. Yes, he's hurt, lying somewhere around here! Why don't you—?"

"Take it easy, Mr. Marker," a police captain said.

Another police captain said, "We're looking, Mr. Marker. We haven't found him yet. There was an explosion, you see? Did you have explosives in there?

"In a chemical plant? Of course there were explosive materials. Extra insurance, damn them. Adam knew that, he wouldn't have done anything—"

A fireman hurried to the group. His face was streaked with soot, and his slicker dripped water. He spoke low to the captain. The fire captain turned to John Marker.

"They've found a body inside, Mr. Marker. Perhaps—"

"A body?" the plant owner said. "He . . . Adam was the only one in there. Just one watchman. He wanted to work. He—"

The red-eyed, smoke-blackened fireman spoke low to the captain again. The fire captain frowned.

"You're sure your son was the only person inside, Mr.

Marker?"

"Of course I'm sure. Would I say—"

"The body's a woman, Mr. Marker," the fire captain said. "A girl, young. Her face is burned, but she's not blown up."

"A girl?" John Marker said, blinked. "That's impossible!"

"Maybe your son took his girl in with him," a police captain said. "Night work, alone, and he's young, right?"

John Marker shook his head. "Adam had no girl. He's a serious boy, mixed up, only home a year." The plant owner stopped, his eyes suddenly brighter. "A girl? Then Adam may still be . . . okay? Somewhere?"

Adam was his son. The dead girl was some stranger.

"We're still looking, Mr. Marker," the fire captain said. "They're bringing the girl. Maybe you do know her."

Two firemen came up carrying a canvas-covered stretcher. The body of the girl was small, like a child on the large stretcher. They uncovered the body for John Marker. The face was charred, but the legs and torso were untouched. Jackson recognized the clothes and the girl—Rosa Brunner.

"No, I don't know her," John Marker said.

The firemen carried the body toward a morgue wagon. Jackson walked out of the crowd. He knew there would be no one else inside the shattered building. The police and firemen didn't, and Jackson wasn't going to tell them. They would find the evidence of the Weatherman group soon enough.

Alone in the flickering shadows of the street, a sudden rage swept over Jackson. An hour ago he had watched Rosa Brunner's small hands shake as she made her bomb, sweat on her pretty young face. Telling her father that she wasn't on drugs, was no danger, would do her job; telling Frank

Walton that she was only nervous—telling Walton because she had been in love with Frank Walton. It had been there in her eyes, her need for Frank Walton, whether the ex-Marine had known it or not. A young girl, a child, desperate to be alive, to please her men, to be part of what her men wanted.

Jackson swore aloud in the night, the dying flames behind him; the red lights of the police cars, and the hot eyes of the curious, all around him. The waste! For what? To make a better world? Who didn't want a better damn world? Most men would kill for a better world, if not so damned many would die for it. Lenin's broken eggs were fine—if you weren't the egg. What about the poor goddamned eggs? Maybe America was hell bent down the wrong road, maybe the whole damned world was, but how many had to die to make the road right? Fifty million more? Sixty million more to match the sixty million killed in the last sixty-odd years in the name of one cause or another? Or only one—Rosa Brunner, the child-victim of fanatic amateurs too arrogant to learn how to do what they were doing?

He looked up from the shadows to the dark window of his room. His rage seemed to gather into a small, hard rock in his belly. Maybe Frank Walton, all of them, knew the right road—but their murderous methods would make it a wide superhighway through an empty land, eight perfect lanes of concrete as far as any eye could see—with no one on it, empty, no eyes left to see its beautiful perfection.

Jackson walked to his rented car in the alley.

The name Jackson wanted was in his small, thick, black-leather address book—Major Saul Gorshin, ex-military intelligence, ex-C.I.A., Gilmore City Council 1966 to present, address . . .

The address was a two-story neo-Colonial house in one of the newer residential sections of Gilmore. It faced the Country Club, looked out over the dark greens of the golf course. At this early morning hour the rich neighborhood was dark among its trees and shrubs and manicured lawns. Only a few isolated lights showed in scattered windows. One of them was in Gorshin's house—a downstairs, corner room.

Jackson parked, walked to the front door. The door opened before he reached it.

"Who the hell is it? Don't you know what time—!"

"Hello, Saul," Jackson said.

Saul Gorshin came out a step, half closed the door. The City Councilman looked around, a kind of reflex action, as if Jackson's voice made him suspect danger in the night.

"What do you want here, Kane?"

"No big welcome, Saul? No long-time-no-see?"

"I know what you're doing now, Kane," Saul Gorshin said. "We've got ways, right? Didn't you get enough dirty work in the service? At least that was for your country, not for money."

"Not all of us can go into politics, Saul."

"Don't tell me the army left you with only one trade! I don't buy that argument. A man can do what he wants in this country!"

"Maybe he can," Jackson said. "I'm not here to debate my life. I'm here to maybe help this country."

"How?"

"Do we talk out here? Think of the neighbors."

"All right, come in—but be quiet, my wife's sleeping."

In the single desk light of Gorshin's study, papers were spread across an ornate, inlaid desk. The trophies and photographs of twenty years were on the walls—twenty years of war, open and secret. Gorshin didn't sit down.

"Well, Kane?"

Jackson told his fellow ex-army spy about the Weatherman group, the explosion, his own impersonation of a Weatherman, and that Frank Walton was waiting to make his escape. He left out his reason for being with the Weathermen, and just where Walton was waiting. Gorshin paced his study, his mouth working like a man chewing some tough, repugnant food.

"A bomb factory? In Gilmore? To blow up what, Kane?"

"An oil refinery. I don't know what refinery or where."

Gorshin stopped pacing. "What do you want me to do?"

"Get me to someone high up enough to keep my name out of it, and I'll turn Frank Walton in, tell all I can about the rest."

"You're sure you're not one of them, Kane?"

"You think I could be?"

Gorshin watched Jackson. "No, I suppose not. Spying is bad training for idealism. How did you fool them?"

"I've got the contacts, you know that."

Gorshin nodded slowly. "What were you doing there with them, Kane?"

"Do you really want to know, Saul?"

"No, I suppose not. I don't want to know."

The Councilman began to pace again. He paced the study for a time while Jackson leaned against a wall. The minutes ticked away on a large mantel clock. Gorshin talked:

"How did we let it happen? Violent, alien ideas injected into our youth like a plague. We've allowed the schools, the colleges, to teach these ideas instead of our own ideas, our way. We've lacked guts and commitment,

Kane. I blame myself as well as every man over forty. We know what we have here, what the truth is, but we were so busy using it that we forgot to pass it on."

He stopped his pacing again. "All right, we'll go to the Chief of Police. Right now. But we'll need some story to explain how you got involved."

"I'm a private detective from Los Angeles," Jackson said. "I was approached to make fuses, and saw my chance to infiltrate the Weathermen. Now I'm reporting. A private patriot."

"That's pretty thin."

"They can't disprove it, and you'll vouch for me. That's why I came to you first, Saul."

"If it's the best you can do," Saul Gorshin said. "Let's go before this Walton gets nervous.

The Chief of the Gilmore Police Department was a dapper man of fifty. In his bathrobe, he wasn't pleased at being routed out of bed. His manner changed as he listened to Councilman Gorshin tell Jackson's story. His eyes were sharp.

"You're a Weatherman, Jackson?"

"I've seen too much to think anything can be helped by a few alienated kids blowing up buildings," Jackson said. "I'm a private detective out of L.A. I happen to have militant connections, Gorshin can tell you why. I saw a chance to infiltrate and took it."

"You expect me to accept just that? No questions?"

"You'll have to, Chief. If you want Walton and the rest."

"No I won't!" the Chief said angrily. "It's a lot more likely that you're one of them trying to cop out. You're turning in your friends to cover yourself. I'm going to hold you, mister."

"Then hold me! But you won't get one of them!"

The Chief reddened. "Don't you try to threaten—"

"Hold it! Both of you!" Councilman Gorshin snapped.

Jackson and the Chief stood almost nose to nose, glaring at each other. The Chief hot, Jackson cool. Councilman Gorshin watched them both.

"Back off, Kane," the former Major said. "Your story sounds phony, and the Chief has his job. But, Chief, maybe Jackson is hiding something, but I'll guarantee that if he is it has no bearing on these terrorists. He's no terrorist or Weatherman, I'll vouch for that. I served with Kane for a lot of years in military intelligence, his record is above suspicion, and you can check it. In any case, it doesn't matter what he was doing with that group. All we need to know is that he's turning in this Frank Walton and the others. That's all that matters now."

The Chief chewed his lip. "I suppose it doesn't matter. I'll take your word, Major. All right, where is this Walton?"

"No," Jackson said. "If you pick him up where he is, he'd know who turned him in. I don't want any suspicion on me."

"Then how the hell do we get him?" the Chief demanded.

"I'll deliver his message to this Raymondo Peña, you can pick them both up when they meet."

"How do we know where they'll meet?"

"I'll tell you," Jackson said, and he outlined his plan for turning-in Frank Walton without Walton guessing who had tipped the police. Gorshin nodded, the Chief looked doubtful.

"It's awful chancy, we could lose him."

"Not if you move right," Jackson said.

"What about the other three?" the Chief asked.

Jackson described Adam Marker, Emil Brunner and Amanda Blake, told how he had last seen them, and described the pickup truck two of them had escaped in. The Chief wrote it all down.

"Why, Jackson?" the Chief said, closed his notebook. "You don't sound like you're really on our side much."

"Maybe I'm on no side," Jackson said. "Let's say I don't like amateurs with bombs. The next accident might blow me up with it. Say I'm looking out for myself, okay?"

"I can believe that," the Chief said.

Councilman Gorshin said nothing. Jackson walked out.

6

Raymondo Peña was a small, skinny Cuban with eyes that never looked at anyone. In his room over the campus bookstore, he listened to Jackson's story, the message from Frank Walton, and nodded.

"Okay. Tell him, okay."

That was all—the Cuban wasn't going to tell Jackson anything about his preplanned arrangement with Frank Walton. Jackson hadn't expected that the Cuban would. In any real underground you trust no one, say as little as possible, and this was a real underground in the country today.

Jackson drove back to the dark street on the outskirts of Gilmore. The crowd of curious was gone, the last firemen hosing down the blackened ruins of Marker Chemical, sifting the debris for any more bodies or clues to what had exploded. They looked as tired as Jackson felt, but he had work still to do.

He circled the block to be sure he hadn't been followed. He didn't quite trust the Chief. But he spotted no tail on him, and finally pulled into the alley beside the rooming house. He went in, and up to his room. He knocked, identified himself, before he went in.

Frank Walton sat in the same chair, his pistol up and aimed at the door. His eyes were heavy, as if he'd been dozing.

"Set?" the tall ex-Marine said.

"Yes."

"No trouble?"

"No. I've got a taxi standing by to take you wherever you're going to meet Peña."

Walton looked at his watch. "Half an hour. No trouble here, but you had a call. No name. A nervous party, a man."

"My cover work," Jackson said, sat down facing the tall revolutionary. "I'm a private detective. I'm tailing a woman for her husband. I always have a reason to be where I am."

"You work for pigs like that?"

"I need a cover."

"No one needs a cover. Come underground. Or are you just a paid hand? That's a lot of equipment you have in that case."

Jackson's quick glance took in the equipment case and the smaller black bag. Both bags had been opened. Frank Walton wouldn't apologize. It was part of being a revolutionary to know everything about anyone you dealt with.

"I hope you were careful with the small bag, it's got fulminate in it," Jackson said, picked up the small bag.

"I know fulminate caps," Walton said.

Without looking, Jackson felt inside the bag. The almost invisible seal on the opening of the secret pocket where the copied documents were was unbroken. Walton had not found the secret pocket. Jackson put the bag down.

"You don't trust anyone, not even a brother Weatherman?"

"I trust no one, especially a brother," Walton said. The ex-Marine laid his pistol in his lap again, closed his eyes. "I'm total, Jackson, I don't exist outside the work. I live unseen, and I'll die unknown until the revolution is won.

If I live until we win, then the world will know me. If I don't, then only I'll ever know I existed. But I know I exist, and that's more than most slaves in this world ever really know."

Jackson had heard it all before. The pure existential fanaticism of the new revolutionary. Illusion or truth? Maybe a little of both. So he said nothing. He waited. Frank Walton sat without opening his eyes, waiting, too, for the time to move. A sense of tired weight hung over the silent room. Each of them silent with his own thoughts. For Jackson it was thoughts of the end of it, finishing it. For Walton it was probably thoughts of the next step, the next attack, going on.

The half an hour passed slowly. Walton had nothing to do but wait, Jackson had finished all he had to do. It was Frank Walton who moved first. He opened his eyes.

"Okay, time," Walton said. "Help me downstairs."

"I'll call my taxi driver."

"No," Frank Walton said. "I'll take your car."

Jackson nodded. "You're careful, but the taxi isn't a trap."

"I didn't say it was, but I never follow a plan made in advance," Walton said. "It's safer that way. Let's go."

The tall ex-Marine shoved his pistol inside his belt, heaved himself to his feet, gritting his teeth against the pain of his leg. Jackson supported him, and they went slowly out into the hall and down the stairs. Outside, Walton got behind the wheel of Jackson's rented car. He started the car.

"Maybe we'll work together again, Jackson," he said.

"Maybe we will," Jackson said.

He stepped back and watched the car drive out into the street where one solitary fire engine still pumped water into the ruins of Marker Chemical. He walked to the mouth of the alley. His car had already vanished around the corner onto the avenue. Jackson waited. The police cars passed in the night on the avenue, heading south, following the signal of the homing device Jackson had attached to his rented car. Frank Walton would lead them straight to his meeting with Raymondo Peña. The Chief would be there to pick up Walton and Peña.

Jackson went back up to the room, picked up his two bags. He smiled a thin smile, he had been right in his judgment of how Frank Walton would act. He had been certain that Walton would avoid the taxi, and take the car at the last minute. It was how he, Jackson, would have acted under the circumstances. So he had attached the homer to his rented car, and the police would have no trouble finding Frank Walton. Of course, he had fixed the taxi, too, just in case.

Now he called the taxi, carried his bags down, and the taxi drove him to a motel on the highway from Gilmore to Los Angeles. He needed a few hours' sleep, and in case anything went wrong, he wasn't going to be in the rooming house if Frank Walton came back.

But Walton wouldn't come back, and Jackson had only one more stop before this job was over.

Edgar Callison motioned Jackson into his inner office in the office skyscraper on Wilshire Boulevard in Los Angeles. The heavy-faced, burly businessman held the morning newspaper.

"Did you blow it, Jackson? Marker's plant?"

Through the high windows downtown Los Angeles towered to the south under its perennial haze in the morning sun. To the west the sea would have been visible except for the haze. An office with two views—the privilege of a company president.

"No," Jackson said.

"Where were you last night, then? I called late, some stranger answered. He tried to pump me. I hung up."

"It's a long story, nothing to do with you," Jackson said. The agent sat down. "I tried to call you about twelve-thirty. No answer, the special number. Where were you?"

"I had some business, private."

"You're sure you didn't decide to put John Marker out of business without waiting for my final report?"

"You think that I—?"

Callison moved away from where he had been standing at his door. He walked behind his desk. He sat down, took out a handkerchief and mopped his face, dried his hands.

"Why would I blow up that plant?"

"You already knew he'd stolen your sales lists, cost figures. You wanted him out of business, without knowing anything else."

"I didn't blow up that plant," Edgar Callison said.

"Can you prove it?"

"Of course, but I won't have to, will I? You won't tell anyone I had any interest in John Marker."

"You've got it figured out."

"Yes, I have. What did you find last night?"

Jackson opened his small bag, took the copied documents from the secret pocket. "He took what looks like complete details of the new adhesive process when he left your company—a photocopy of the full report, it looks like to me." He gave the six-page document to Callison, who stared at it. "Then he has two of your top scientists, the two who worked with him when he was with you developing the adhesive, signed to go with him as soon as he pays them a five-thousand-dollar bonus, plus almost doubling their salaries."

Callison took the two single sheets. He looked at them in fury. "Klein and Unger! Two of my best men. The damned pirate! I'll break Marker, so help me I'll—"

"He's broken already."

"The explosion? He'll be insured. All it'll cost is—"

"Insurance?"

"Of course, but if he was ready to start operation, he'll just about break even. He'll lose time, maybe a year, and that will cost him. But he's not broken yet. I'll handle that, and I'll take care of Doctors Klein and Unger. The rotten traitors!"

"You've got the time to stop him now."

Callison almost smiled. "I do, don't I?"

"Lucky, that explosion," Jackson said. "Okay, you can pay me now, and that's it. Total is seventy-five hundred above the advance check. Here are the details, mostly bribes to my contacts."

Callison read over the bill. "All right, you did the job."

Callison wrote out the check, while Jackson tore up the bill, dropped it into a wastebasket. Callison handed him the check. Jackson pocketed it, stood up.

"You need me again, you know how to call me," he told the businessman. "Remember, this never happened. I can prove I was somewhere else, if I have to. And I can prove you hired me to spy, if I have to."

Edgar Callison nodded. Jackson picked up his small bag and left the private office with its vast, hazy view out over Los Angeles. He hated the city with its arrogant strut and hungry eyes, the job was finished, and he could get home to his mountainside house and do nothing but sit in the sun for a week.

He rode the elevator down to the parking garage, and drove the car he had rented this morning to where he turned it in. He took a taxi to where he had left his Mercedes over two weeks ago. He changed into a dark green blazer, open shirt, and slim gray slacks, packed his pistol in his equipment case, locked the case and his small bag into the trunk, and drove to the Ventura Freeway.

At Oxnard he began to relax, and when he had passed through Ventura into the green, lush coastland, he began to think of his woman, Kate Chapman, and changed his time doing nothing from a week to a month.

7

Jackson got four days.

One day in his glass-and-redwood house with Kate Chapman, the woman he had met on a case in Ohio, who had come to visit for a vacation, and who had stayed. Three days sailing, swimming, drinking, talking and sleeping—with Kate Chapman. No more.

On the fourth day he went to check his mail at his Santa Barbara office suite in the building that looked more like some hotel on the Riviera set among flowers, grass and palms. His office had the simple label: Kane Jackson Associates, Industrial Consultants. His inner office was locked tight and windowless. The outer office was an ordinary reception room and secretarial office, except that there was no secretary unless he hired one for a few special days, and no one ever waited in the reception room. Today, someone did.

He was an ordinary man in a stained gray hat and worn suit. His face was thick and flat, his eyes small and quick. There was a faint bulge under his left arm. He smiled.

"Nice office you got here. It was hot, so I came in."

Jackson crossed to the secretary's desk and sat down. He lit one of his cigars. He didn't ask how the man had gotten in.

"That's some lock on your inside door," the man went on. "No way I could open that one. Interesting. I guess we don't talk in there, no? Tell me, are you a detective or a consultant?"

"Both," Jackson said. "I like money. What are you? Captain? Lieutenant? L.A.P.D.?"

"Just sergeant," the man said, rubbed his jaw. "The gun and the cheap suit does it, right? Not rich enough to be a hood. You can tell right off what I am."

Jackson said nothing.

"Now you, it's not so easy to tell what you are," the police sergeant went on. "I've had some days to check. That little office in Inglewood with the slick phone-answering setup, very interesting. No way of tracing where the messages really end up, right? You've got a private license, that Inglewood address in L.A., but the L.A.P.D. doesn't know much about you. No one knows much about you. I run into dead ends everywhere. This office, for instance—no secretary, no windows in that inside office, nothing to say what you consult about, and no other 'consultants' I can see. As far as I can see you don't work much, but you live good. I figure you're more than you seem, you know?"

Jackson said, "You're not a Los Angeles cop?"

"Gilmore. Sergeant Prather."

"I've got no more interest in Gilmore. I told the Chief."

"Yeh," Sergeant Prather said. "We picked up Frank Walton and Raymondo Peña that night. No trace of the others."

"They won't be in Gilmore now."

"That's how we figure, too," Sergeant Prather said, nodded. "Gone underground, and that's going to make them hard to find. We want them, we figure you could help us."

"No," Jackson said.

Sergeant Prather said, "Three days I've been checking—

L.A. cops, Frisco, Portland, Seattle, the F.B.I. I tell you, that cover of yours is so good no one would ever believe you're not a real Weatherman. Not without a lot of proof from you."

"I'm no Weatherman, and you know it."

"Maybe," Prather agreed. "Maybe I know you're not a simple private detective, either. Now that's hard to prove, too, it'd take me a long time, even with Councilman Gorshin helping me out. But I know your military record, the part that isn't still classified, and I can guess what you really do. I've even got a hunch why you were in Gilmore, and not to chase Weathermen."

"Why would Saul Gorshin help you?"

"He knows we need those other three Weathermen, and you've got the best chance to get to them for us. Our only chance, maybe."

"Why do you need them?"

"Well, there's the explosion. It's just possible it wasn't an accident. No proof yet, but we're working. Then there's the Brunner girl."

"What about her?"

"Seems she didn't die in the explosion," Prather said. "Seems she was murdered."

Jackson smoked. "How?"

"Stabbed. Some long, thin knife. Docs say it had to have happened before the fire or the explosion. Maybe the explosion was set off for cover, you know? We figure it had to have been one of that Weatherman group. You know them."

Jackson knew them. He remembered the tensions in the group, the open antagonisms, the problem of Rosa Brunner.

Sergeant Prather said, "We haven't got much chance to get the killer. But you can go back underground, you've got the cover and the contacts, and dig us out a killer."

"No," Jackson said. "Don't con me, Sergeant. Now you can stay here if you want, I'm going."

Jackson started for the outside door. Sergeant Prather spoke behind him:

"Where you going, Jackson? I mean, where do you go if I blow your whole cover? If we find out what you were really doing in Gilmore?"

Jackson stopped. "What was I doing?"

"I don't know exactly, I don't really care. But I think we could find out. I think we could blow your whole operation. We can also give you to the F.B.I. as a Weatherman. You'll never prove you're not a Weatherman without telling what you really are. One way or the other, you've got nowhere to go unless you go to work for us."

"A spy for you in the underground?"

"No one could do it better," Prather said, smiled. "Saul Gorshin says no one could do it better."

"What about Frank Walton?"

"We don't think he suspects you turned him in. Just in case, we'll hold him as long as we can. If he gets bailed out, or a writ, you'll have to keep ahead of him."

"What help do I get?"

"In Gilmore, all you need. Anywhere else, on your own."

Jackson thought. "She was stabbed?"

"Straight murder," Sergeant Prather said.

"I'll be in touch," Jackson said.

After Sergeant Prather had gone, Jackson sat for a time in the outer office. His underground cover was good, but how good? For one group over three days, yes. But how long would it hold moving around openly from group to group? He didn't know, but he got up and went out to his car, and drove toward his house on the mountain to tell

Kate Chapman that he was going back to work a lot sooner than he had expected.

As he drove he remembered his rage at the death of Rosa Brunner. He felt it again. A more private rage.

Someone was a private killer now.

Part Two

Part Two

8

After two days of telephone calls, telegrams, and waiting, Jackson had nothing. None of his contacts could tell him where Adam Marker, Emil Brunner, or Amanda Blake were. Frank Walton had been questioned around the clock in Gilmore, before they told him they knew Rosa Brunner had been murdered, and after they told him. Sergeant Prather had nothing to report, except that Frank Walton knew every angle of the law.

Time was running out, the three fugitives could be in Cuba within days—if they weren't already. One of them, at least.

Jackson got back into his army fatigues, put on his little Mauser, packed his equipment bag, rented a car, and drove south toward Gilmore.

Into their world.

John Marker's house was a run-down mansion in a wooded section of Gilmore north of the railroad yards. Built by the blunt businessmen of an earlier era who liked to look on their own works and find them good, the house had a clear view of the smoking railroad yards. A large swimming pool had an abandoned air despite the September heat, and a woman in a bikini lying beside it in the distance. Weeds grew all around the pool, and in the large grounds, giving it all a sense of transience.

Jackson rang twice and waited some minutes before a blond woman opened the door. She was small and slender, and wore a blue terrycloth robe. There was a good figure under the robe, and her pretty face was warm and smiling. About thirty.

"I'd like to see Mr. Marker," Jackson said.

"Johnny? He is not here. I am Mrs. Marker. He will be here soon, I think. You would like to wait?"

Her soft, pleasant voice had an Italian accent.

"Thanks, I will," Jackson said.

She stepped back with a big smile as if doing things for people, maybe for men, pleased her, and led him through the big house toward the rear. Most of the rooms looked dusty and unused, furnished with heavy old pieces going a little shabby, but the rear living room had a different feel. It was lived in, cared for, furnished with light, Italian provincial furniture not like the rest of the rooms. Mrs. Marker saw Jackson looking.

"From my home, this," she smiled, waved at the Italian furniture. "A nice room, full of sun. In Italy our house it was always sunny, full of people." Her face was wistful.

"The three of you live here alone?" Jackson asked.

"Only two," Mrs. Marker said. "Adam was with us when he came from prison, but he left."

They were out on the cement terrace now. Weeds grew among the cracks in the cement, and at the edge of the big pool. Some weeds had been pulled by hand. Mrs. Marker smiled.

"Sometimes I must destroy the weeds, but I am lazy, the sun is hot, the pool is so blue—" she shrugged lightly. "But we will not stay here now, I think. Johnny enjoys it in Los Angeles better. You are a friend of Johnny?"

"Of Adam," Jackson said. "I thought he would be here."

She shook her head, the thick mane of blond hair flowing in the sun. "He lived with us only a little time. He is a man, he has his own apartment."

"No other children, Mrs. Marker?"

"You mean from me?" she said, smiled again. "No. Perhaps sometime, who knows, yes? Children are, what do you say, a . . . a . . . by-product, yes, of marriage. A marriage is a man and a woman, they make the life for each other. Johnny makes me a good life, I please him, make his friends welcome. Yes?"

"Sounds fine," Jackson grinned. "You've been married long?"

"Three years. My employer in Italy came to Los Angeles on business. I meet Johnny. My employer was very angry. Johnny was a . . . a . . . His wife was dead?"

"Widower," Jackson said.

"Yes, widower. We marry. He does not like to live in his old house. Very small, not a nice house."

"He was working for Edgar Callison when you met?"

"Yes. He has his own company only six months. Now—" she shrugged again. "The insurance will pay, but it is not enough for what is lost. Still, Johnny enjoys Los Angeles better, we will—"

Jackson had heard the car drive up some minutes earlier. He had been listening for anyone approaching. He had never met John Marker, but the businessman might have seen him at the fire, or Adam could have mentioned him. So he wanted to face Marker suddenly when he came in and see any reaction. He didn't turn at once as he heard the man come out onto the terrace.

"What do I enjoy better in Los Angeles, Christina?"

"Everything, Johnny, yes?" She laughed.

"Not everything," John Marker said. "I enjoy you anywhere."

The handsome businessman walked to her, put his arms around her small, slim body. She raised on her toes to kiss him. He stroked her soft shoulders under the blue robe.

"I'm a lucky man," John Marker said to Jackson's back. "But did you want to see me, Mr.—?"

"Kane Jackson," the agent said, and turned.

He watched John Marker, but there seemed to be no reaction. Not to his name, or to his face, or to both together. There was a reaction to Jackson's clothes. John Marker looked him up and down, and something happened in the man's eyes—a frown.

"Take your swim, Christina, all right?" John Marker said.

The small blonde nodded to Jackson, and walked away to the deep end of the big pool. Jackson watched as she dropped the robe—almost shyly. The bikini she wore was not intended for anyone but her husband. A simple woman with a magnificent body, but not a tease, not out for all men's eyes. Jackson hadn't seen that for a long time. Most women seemed to display their bodies and their clothes for other women first, the approval of every man they met second, their own ego third, and for their husbands last. Even Cassie, his ex-wife—we're products of our time.

"I don't know you, Jackson," John Marker said.

"I'm looking for Adam," Jackson said. "You know where he is?"

"No," John Marker said.

The businessman exploded the word, spat it out. His handsome face seemed to twist into a grimace of anger and distaste. He studied Jackson, up and down again, and a kind of light came into his eyes—an angry light.

"By God," he said, "you're one of them! Yes! You've got a lot of gall, you punk!"

"One of what, Marker," Jackson said.

"Them! Those criminals! A bomb factory in my plant! The police told me. You blew up my plant, my company! My own son!"

Jackson said, "All right, you're mad. But where is he, Marker? Adam. I have to find him."

"To blow up more factories? No! The police, that's who I'll help find him!" John Marker began to walk in a small, furious circle on the sunny terrace. "He came here every week! He took a job in my plant! Never a hint of what he was really doing. A terrorist! In *my* plant! Now you come—"

"Why did you give him the job?"

John Marker swore. "Christ, he needed work, he said. Two years in prison because he wouldn't go into the army, where could he work? A pacifist! I didn't agree with him, but I was proud of his stand. A pacifist—making bombs!" The businessman turned on Jackson. "You, all of you. You did it. I know you. You're no kid. Who pays you? Havana? Peking?"

"Where is Adam, Marker? He's in trouble, I have to find—"

"Trouble? You bet he's in trouble! Good! I have no son, you hear? He used me. You're all common criminals! I won't stand here and talk to you. The police—"

The businessman turned and almost stumbled in his haste and anger. Jackson sensed what Marker had in mind —the police. He jumped, hit the man once in the jaw. Marker went down and lay still. In the pool the blond wife screamed. Jackson ran to the pool. She was climbing out to run to her husband. Jackson grabbed her, water dripping on him. She fought.

"He's all right. I want Adam, you understand? He has an apartment, where?"

She struggled, gave up, glared up at him. "Number 16, Rio Negre Street. You—"

"Where else would he go?"

"I don't know! Let me go to—"

"Where else!" Jackson demanded, held her. Her full breasts pressed against him, big and soft. She recoiled, had to escape.

"I don't know! A . . . a . . . Brunner. Yes, Emil Brunner, a friend he talk about. Cortez Way, 27, yes. Now—"

Jackson let her go. John Marker was moving on the cement terrace. She bent over the businessman. Jackson went out through the big, dusty house to his car.

Jackson didn't expect to find Adam Marker at the apartment at 16 Rio Negre Street. He didn't. He unlocked the door with his ring of keys. The two small, shabby rooms were almost bare, and completely empty of anything personal. It didn't look like Adam Marker had spent much time here, unless he had stopped on the night of the explosion to clean it out.

He found only one item—a woman's lipstick; an expensive lipstick. It had been bought in a Detroit store from the small label still attached at the bottom.

Jackson took it when he left.

Cortez Way was in a lower-middle-class tract of curving streets a half mile from the railroad yards. The identical small houses were built close together in what had been a flat, dusty field. Jackson parked in front of number 27.

A very tall, skinny man came out of number 27. He walked in long, slouching strides to a five-year-old Ford parked in the driveway. His suit hung on him like a scarecrow, one bony shoulder lower than the other, his big hands dangling at the end of long arms. As Jackson got out of the car, the tall, skinny man paused and looked back at the industrial agent. Jackson walked toward him. The man got into his Ford quickly, drove out into the quiet street and away.

Jackson watched the Ford go, then turned back to the house. A silence hung over number 27, its shades all drawn. Death had struck here, but Jackson sensed that the silence had begun before Rosa Brunner had died. Its lawn was ragged with bare patches, only vaguely mowed. The shrubs, green at the other houses, were dry and brown. The house itself needed paint. A single old Chevvy sedan was in the car port. Jackson went to the front door.

For a long time there was no answer to his ringing. On the sunny street children played. He heard nothing inside the house, yet the skinny man had come out. Someone had to be inside, unless the skinny man . . . ?

"Mrs. Brunner? Emil?" Jackson called out in the silence.

The children up the hot street stopped playing to stare at Jackson. He heard something move inside. Not far inside the door, as if someone was sitting just inside waiting for him to go away. There was a slow shuffling, and the door opened on a woman with flat eyes and a worn face that wasn't old but that would never be young again, either.

"What do you want?" she said.

She was about forty, probably younger, and had been pretty. Her face was fine-boned, and smile wrinkles were still visible under the harsh downward lines that dominated her face now.

"I want Emil, Mrs. Brunner," Jackson said.

"He's not here. Go away."

"Let's talk about it," Jackson said, pushed inside.

Mrs. Brunner didn't stop him. She walked back into a small living room and sat down in a bentwood rocker. Jackson closed the outside door, sat down facing her. She stroked the arm of the old chair, looked down at the chair as if just seeing it.

"We bought this when she was four years old, Rosa. Emil had just come out of jail that time. My back was hurting me, Emil bought the chair for me. One of the Detroit apartments, when Emil was with the Trotsky group. He went to Cuba the next year to work with some of his old Spanish War people. Rosa was eight when he came back that time. She was always proud of him, wanted to please him. I wanted a chair and a place. I made him buy this house so she'd go to high school like other kids. I made him stay home. Maybe I was wrong."

"Where is Emil, Mrs. Brunner?"

"Running and hiding, where else would he be? For the Cause. Any Cause, what difference are the labels, the manifestos? As long as it was violent, destroy the system. Guns, bombs." She looked up at Jackson. "She's dead. Rosa."

"I'm sorry, Mrs. Brunner. They were amateurs, except Emil and me. Some mistake. I wasn't there when—"

"There?" Her eyes darkened as if the dim room behind the shades had gone black. "You're one of the group? And you came here? Don't any of you care who you hurt? Who you pull down with you? You—"

"I wasn't there when it blew, they don't know me. No one—"

"They've got Walton. Spies everywhere!"

She stood up, walked to a chest of drawers in a corner. When she turned she had the pistol in her hand.

"Get out!"

The pistol was aimed straight at Jackson's chest.

9

Jackson stood. "Walton won't tell them anything. I'm an out-of-town expert. I'm not known, and I have to find Emil."

"No! Get out, get away from me. Emil isn't—"

Jackson moved suddenly. He had her arm. She resisted for only a moment, then went limp. He took the gun, laid it on a table. She sat down where she was, on a shabby couch.

"No one finds Emil," she said, her voice abstract again, barely in the dim, neglected room. "Twenty years, I never found him, did I? The Cause. The hundred movements he spent his life fighting for. All one movement—the new world, the perfect world that's going to make everyone happy, content. Everyone. Happy."

"We all want that," Jackson said.

"At first," the woman said, "I worked with him. Back there after the war. It was exciting, a purpose. I followed him from city to city, country to country. No place of our own, we didn't need that, unimportant. We had the Cause. That was home, our place. Warm and cosy, all comrades and brothers."

She rocked on the old couch, hugging herself as if in pain. Birth pain, and death pain.

"Poor Rosa," she said. "She wanted to be like him. She wanted to be heroic. Like Frank Walton."

The woman began to cry. For the girl who had grown up to die for the Cause. One of Lenin's eggs. Nameless, unknown in any history book, not even a line in some pamphlet. An unknown martyr without a statue, but Jackson knew that Mrs. Brunner wasn't crying for the martyr, not even if there had been a statue. She was crying for the child she remembered coming home from school, and Jackson wasn't even in the room for her.

"She was in love with Frank Walton?" he said.

"Love?" Mrs. Brunner said. "Yes, she was in love."

"Did Rosa take drugs?"

"Drugs? No, only the drug of the Cause."

"You're sure?"

She looked up. "Drugs? Rosa? No, I . . . I . . . don't know."

"How long was she in the movement?"

"How long? All her life," Mrs. Brunner said, dried her eyes. "What else would she be part of with Emil for her father, me for her mother? The normal world for her. Born to it. But she never really understood. She pleased her father, then she pleased Frank Walton, tried to. A girl falls in love with a man she meets. Who could Rosa meet except Frank Waltons? But she was never really aware. There was a time when I thought she might reject it all. In high school. She tried to think, to understand for herself. I thought she might oppose . . . But she wasn't strong. She couldn't oppose Emil, or Walton, or any of them. Poor Rosa."

"She could have been against the movement?" Jackson said. "Mrs. Brunner? Could she have been a spy? Informer?"

The woman's head jerked up. "Spy? Rosa?" She watched Jackson. She had been in the revolutionary world all her adult life. "What do you know? Tell me!"

Jackson told her about the stabbing, the murder.

"Killed?" Mrs. Brunner said. "Rosa? Murder?"

"She didn't die in the explosion. Was she an informer?"

The woman said nothing. As if Jackson had already left. She sat silent, seeing some scene, some face, inside. A face, a scene, of horror, from the darkness of her eyes.

"Emil?" Jackson said. "If she was a spy?"

"No," Mrs. Brunner said. "Not Rosa. Not even for the Cause."

But, for a moment, there was something in her voice that said she didn't believe her own words. For the Cause, what wouldn't Emil Brunner do? A spy? Even, maybe, a girl using drugs and so a danger? His own daughter?

"No," Mrs. Brunner said, firm now, the moment past. "Who killed my child? She was no spy, no informer. Frank Walton? A cold animal. The other one, the boy? Adam? He—"

"Adam Marker was in love with Rosa," Jackson said. "She wanted Walton. Jealousy?"

She was silent for a time. "We're equal in the movement, all women. We're soldiers the same as men, but they see our breasts, too, the men. Our breast size is important, our legs, they have their needs, too, revolutionary men."

"And women?" Jackson said. "Is Amanda Blake in love with Frank Walton too? Jealous?"

"Yes, Amanda is Walton's woman. Rosa thought it was over, that she could have Walton. She told me. You think—?"

"It happens," Jackson said.

"Yes," Mrs. Brunner said, her eyes distant now.

"Where can I find Emil, Mrs. Brunner? Someone killed Rosa, inside the movement. We've got to know."

"I don't know. He sent me a message. He can't come to the . . . funeral. No, the Cause demands!"

"A message? Who brought it?"

"Gerhard Myers, an old friend from the Spanish days."

"Where do I find him?"

"North Hollywood. Los Angeles. Number 142 Ensenada Court."

"Is there anything else you can tell me? Where Adam Marker or Amanda Blake are?"

"No."

"A man was here before me, tall and skinny."

"He said he was an insurance investigator."

"What did he want to know?"

"What Rosa was doing in the building. Who else was with her. Where the others were now. I told him nothing. We don't talk to investigators, do we? In the movement."

"No," Jackson said. "If Emil gets in touch, call this number and tell me. Leave a message if I'm not there."

He wrote down his Inglewood office number. She took it, but she didn't look at it. On the couch she began to rock again, her eyes distant as if walking down the paths of her life.

In his car, Jackson looked back at the small house with its dry, neglected lawn and garden. Emil Brunner had more important things in his life than a house or garden. More important than a wife—or a daughter? A daughter on drugs? A daughter who had known too much, and had told?

He released his brake—and saw the Ford in his rearview mirror. The same old Ford the skinny man had driven away. It was parked behind him far up the street. Jackson thought it was the same Ford, and yet? There seemed to be no one in it.

He let his eyes search slowly around the street and the small, quiet houses in the sun. He saw nothing. The children still played up the street. Jackson sat back as if he were going to watch the Brunner house. He kept his eyes on the rearview mirror. Ten minutes passed. No one approached the empty Ford. Then he saw the movement.

Something moved inside the Ford—in the back seat. An old trick to make the car seem empty. Every spy and detective soon learns that people look automatically at the front seat of a parked car, and if it is empty assume that the car is empty. The skinny man could be an insurance investigator after all. Only who was he watching now?

Jackson started his car, made a U-turn, and drove past the parked Ford and on in the opposite direction. In his mirror he watched to see if the Ford would follow. It didn't. It was still parked as Jackson went out of sight around a curve of the tract road. The man was watching the Brunner house.

So the skinny man was an insurance investigator. Then was there some trouble with John Marker's insurance claim? Something special, private, or some clause about acts of war or riot the insurance company was trying to use to get out of paying? Trespassers not covered? Or were the Weathermen trespassers since Adam Marker had let them inside? It . . .

Jackson stopped thinking. The tract drive had curved around to the main road out of the tract. He suddenly realized that there had been no through streets to turn off into, he had been forced to follow the single road until it reached the main exit road at a full stop.

The black Ford was parked hidden behind some trees just to Jackson's left.

The skinny man knew the tract. He had known that

Jackson would have to come to this corner. There had been no need to follow Jackson, only to drive to this corner and wait. The skinny man was following him.

Jackson gave no sign of having seen the Ford. He turned right out of the tract and toward the Freeway to Los Angeles. The Ford was behind him as he pulled onto the Freeway and joined the flow of traffic moving west. Twilight settled over the moving river of cars as Jackson passed through San Bernardino and joined U.S. 10, the San Bernardino Freeway, toward Los Angeles and the coast. The Ford was still behind him.

It was dark as the traffic blended into the Hollywood Freeway north. He couldn't be sure the Ford was behind him after that, but he had a hunch that it was. The skinny man seemed to know his work. When Jackson went down the off-ramp into North Hollywood, a car wasn't far behind him.

Number 142 Ensenada Court was one of those run-down apartment courts that litter half the streets in Hollywood and North Hollywood. Built in the thirties when Los Angeles was in its first violent growth spurt, they all looked the same—squat, semidetached units that looked like old adobe pueblos, all pink or yellow, thin stucco on chicken wire that cracked in a few years, almost unheated inside because in those days Los Angeles had been a mirage where it never rained, was never cold.

Jackson parked openly, walked into the court. A grassy center lawn was bordered by walks on either side. The grass was burned, and the concrete walks were cracked. That wouldn't matter to those who lived here. They would have what they needed—cheap rents. Rents cheap enough to leave them money for their clothes and cars so that they would not know they were failures.

Jackson moved along the rows of semidetached cottages until he found what he wanted—a door with a large, engraved business card over the bell: Gerhard Myers, European Market Consultant, and in smaller letters at the bottom, Translator. Jackson did not ring. He looked behind him. No one was in sight. He ducked around the next unit nearer to the street. He moved lightly along behind the unit until he reached the corner where he could see the front walks.

The tall, skinny man passed under the feeble court lights. Jackson stepped softly to the walk, came up behind the tall man. Close, the man was even taller than he had seemed —six feet six at least, less than a hundred and sixty pounds. A dark-suited praying mantis, his shoulder down and forward, a small head that seemed to bend on its thin neck. The man heard Jackson, turned.

"What do you want with me?" Jackson said.

He looked up into a sharp face with tiny, close-set eyes, and a narrow mouth between a thin nose like a bird's beak and a pointed, receding chin. A black hat worn so low it almost hid the glitter of the small eyes. The man said nothing.

"You tailed me from Gilmore. Why?" Jackson said.

Without a word, the tall skeleton moved straight at Jackson to push past to the street. Walking, not hurrying. Jackson hit the man with his shoulder. The thin giant staggered, almost fell, still made no sound at all.

"What's your interest in the Brunners? In the others?" Jackson said. "You're no insurance investigator."

The skinny man recovered his balance. His long fingers went inside his suit. Jackson saw the glint of the pistol in the weak court light. He hit the man on the jaw. The man went down like a reed bending, all arms and legs flailing, the gun clattering away on the concrete walk.

The man lay for a moment, then slowly struggled up like someone who has been hit before. He still said nothing, made no sound. He had been hit before, he would be hit again, and it made no difference to his actions—what he did was decided by other considerations. Silent, cool, controlled—and hard. He brushed off his suit, looked around for his pistol—and saw something that made him suddenly straighten, as alert as the praying mantis he resembled. Jackson looked, warily.

Someone stood in the doorway of Gerhard Myers' cottage looking at Jackson and the skinny man. The cottage was dark, the man standing there was only a shadow. But a shadow that was somehow familiar to Jackson. Small, thin. There and gone, the door closed, but as the shape vanished the face had come into the beam of a court light for an instant—Adam Marker.

Jackson turned to the skinny man. "We'll go inside, and—"

The skeletal giant held a pistol. Another gun, the big one still lying on the cement. A small gun, a spare, and that told Jackson a lot about the skinny giant's work. It didn't tell what the man was going to do with the small gun.

The man did nothing. He circled Jackson, picked up his big pistol, holstered it under his arm, and backed away out of the court. He still hadn't made a sound. A man who was going to give nothing away.

Jackson didn't follow him. The skinny man handled himself too well to be caught easily again, and Jackson had other matters on his mind now. He went to the door of Gerhard Myers' cottage, rang the bell.

There was no answer.

"Adam? It's Jackson. Open up."
Silence.
"Adam?"

Jackson pushed at the door. It was open. He went inside.

10

Adam Marker sat in the dark living room. The weak light from outside outlined his pale hands in his lap, the dull shine of his eyes staring straight ahead.

"Marker?" Jackson said.

The youth didn't answer, his head sunk on his thin shoulders, his face brooding.

"Where's Gerhard Myers?" Jackson said.

"I don't know."

"What are you doing here? Looking for Emil Brunner?"

"Yes," Adam Marker said, looked up. "Where is he?"

"I'm looking for him too."

Adam nodded. "Dead, Rosa. She's dead, blown up. How?"

"I was across the street, I saw."

"We all got out, not hurt," the youth said. "Rosa didn't. Why didn't she get out? No one else was hurt."

"Walton broke his leg."

Adam Marker didn't seem to hear. "He was first out, Emil was. He ran first. Left us. I found Amanda, she was all right. We got to the truck. I just drove. All night." The youth turned his whole head to fix his eyes on Jackson. "He ran, Emil. He didn't even stop to cry for her!"

"Where would he go, Adam?"

"I just drove all night," Adam Marker said to the room, the darkness. "Amanda left, I just drove. We were rehearsing the attack, the refinery. I was out in the corridor. It blew up, the whole place! I was on the floor. The roof held, the corridor held. I tried to find them, saw Emil run out the front. Amanda was in the small lab. I couldn't find Walton. I . . . I found Rosa. Dead. She was dead! How?"

"Bombs aren't toys," Jackson said.

Adam Marker sat silent in the chair in the dark cottage room. The heavy traffic on the two near freeways seemed to move the night and the darkness itself with the steady, endless hissing rumble of a million tires. Slowly, the youth raised his hands to his eyes and pressed.

"God, I'm so tired." He dropped his hands, let them rest limp in his lap. "Sometimes I feel I can't move, not ever. I ache. Everywhere. So tired."

"Was Rosa using drugs, Adam?" Jackson said.

"No! Walton was crazy! Not Rosa. She was so scared all the time. She never should have been there!"

"Could she have been a spy, an informer?"

Adam Marker's head jerked up, around. "No! Who ever said that Rosa—"

"She wasn't killed by that explosion, Adam. She was stabbed, murdered—before the explosion."

The youth's eyes were like ghosts. "How do you know?"

"We've got ways to get what the police know."

"Murdered? Rosa?" Adam Marker shook his head back and forth like a dog shaking off water, his head almost loose on his neck. "Why? Who? One of—?"

"Who else was there?"

Adam blinked. For a moment in the silence of the dark room he said nothing. He shook his head again, back and forth.

"You think that one of us—?" he said. "Because she was a spy? No, never."

"Personal, then? You were in love with her."

"Me? Yes, I loved her! She wanted Walton! Amanda had Walton, she . . . No, none of us!" The youth hunched forward in the chair, his eyes were wet, almost crying. "She got me in the Weathermen, Rosa did. I met her after I got out of jail. She took me to Emil. He made me see that America was becoming worse and worse. There wasn't any hope of change through the simpler, more peaceful means I'd tried. So I joined. Rosa made me join. She could never work against her father. She was nice to me then, at first, until Walton came. She—"

His voice trailed off, his feverish eyes at some point low on the far wall. Jackson watched the militant youth with the thin, intense shoulders bent forward.

"Could the explosion have been rigged, Adam? Set off?"

"By us? We could all have been killed."

"You weren't. No one was, not by the explosion. Where did it go off? Do you remember?"

"No. I'm not sure. It happened so fast. Far from where I was. Behind the big lab, maybe, the storeroom where we kept some dynamite and plastic."

"Was anyone else there? A stranger, but someone who Rosa knew? Someone Rosa recognized?"

"Recognized? You mean—someone setting the bombs off?"

"Yes."

"Someone Rosa knew." The tone of Adam Marker's voice was more an answer than a question.

Jackson guessed. "Did your father know Rosa?"

"Yes, he knew her. At least, they met once. I took Rosa to the house once, and—" Even in the dark the youth's face was ashen, almost yellow. "I . . . I'm sick."

He stood, held to the chair, walked stiffly into the

next room holding his mouth. Jackson followed him. He watched the youth go into the bathroom, the sound of retching. Water began to run. A revolutionist who hid the sound of vomiting with running water. The paradox of today—well-mannered bombers.

Jackson went back to the living room, began to look around. There was little to see. A simple furnished room with few personal marks of its present occupant. The endless rooms where little men all over the world left no mark of their passage.

The alarm in his head became aware of a change. Water still ran in the bathroom, but there was no other sound. He walked into the bedroom, pushed the bathroom door open.

The bathroom window was raised.

Adam Marker was gone.

Jackson was still swearing at himself when he reached his car. He had an idea where Adam was going, and climbed in behind the steering wheel fast. It was his second mistake within five minutes.

"Keep your hands on the wheel."

The voice came from his back seat. Jackson saw the face shadowy in his rearview mirror—the tall, skinny man. The voice said that the man had his gun.

"You can talk," Jackson said. "You have a name, too?"

"Marty Klegg. Drive ahead, left at the corner."

"Where do we go?"

"Where I'm getting paid to take you. Right a block up."

The skinny man directed him. They took the freeway, and went off in downtown Los Angeles. They stopped in the garage under the Carleton Hotel—one of the new and best. As they went up in the elevator, Klegg put his gun away. Jackson made no move. He wanted to see where he was going, and, then, he didn't think Marty Klegg would hesitate a second to hit him even in front of a crowd.

The room on the sixth floor was opened by an imposing man in a gray suit. Jackson had never seen the man before. The gray suit hung so smoothly it barely rippled when he moved, as if hidden devices connected it to his skin.

"Come in, Jackson," the well-tailored man said.

Jackson went in with Klegg right behind him. The imposing man closed the door, turned to Jackson.

"I'm Robert Blake. You were with my daughter in that place. I want to know where she is."

Robert Blake was under six feet tall, but he stood like a man who considered himself a giant. His hair was thick and barely graying, shining and brushed, and his face was almost too handsome in a smooth-yet-rugged way—like those square-jawed Yale men in shirt ads of the twenties. His voice had the kind of dynamic confidence Jackson had heard before from businessmen so successful that being elected U.S. Senator was something of a comedown in power circles. The kind of man who dominates a board of directors, could probably command an army in his spare time, but who can get down in the dirt and take apart his own car if necessary.

"I don't know where she is," Jackson said. "I'm looking for her too. Your hired hand was trailing Emil Brunner. You have reason to think she could be with him?"

"We ask the questions, Jackson," Marty Klegg said.

"Be quiet, Klegg," Robert Blake said. He didn't raise his voice, he probably never did. People jumped anyway. He moved from the door, sat down. "I don't know who she may be with, Jackson. With that Walton in jail, Brunner was the only one of you Klegg felt he could perhaps trace."

"How long have you been after Amanda?" Jackson said.

A movement at the far end of the hotel room caught his eye. A woman stood so still in a flowered dress that she was almost invisible against flowered drapes. She was half turned looking out through a break in the drapes, but there was only darkness outside. A woman almost as tall as Robert Blake himself, thick in the middle but far from really heavy, her gray hair worn in short, soft waves around a serene face. Her face would never show any tension, but her hands twisted together where she stood. Perhaps fifty, about Blake's age. She had moved to look toward Jackson.

"A long time, Mr. Jackson," she said. "We've been looking for Amanda for years, off and on. This time for a month. We're worried. We hired Mr. Klegg to help us this time."

"My wife speaks figuratively, Jackson," Robert Blake said. "We've always known where Amanda was, even if she was alienated from us. Only for some two months have we been unable to contact her. We hired Klegg, he's a detective, and he traced her to Gilmore and your group."

"Klegg traced her to the Marker Chemical plant?"

"I traced her there," Klegg said.

Robert Blake was up again. "That day, Jackson. The day it blew up! Before we had a chance to reach her! We never knew she was involved—"

"We knew, Robert." The wife, Mrs. Blake, walked farther into the room, away from her window. "We knew what she was doing, that's why we had to find her."

"We didn't know her life was in danger, Celia!" Blake said.

Celia Blake shook her head. "We knew, Robert. We tried not to know. There were checks, Mr. Jackson. Her dividend checks, checks from her trust fund. They came back endorsed by radical organizations, arms companies, explosives companies. We knew."

Robert Blake sat down again. As if there was no way he could be easy, nowhere he could stand or sit. "The last check was from San Francisco, it had a name on it, Frank Walton, as well as the endorsement of an explosives house. We went to San Francisco, looked for a detective who might know a Frank Walton. Klegg did."

Klegg leaned on a wall. "Walton's known up in the Bay Area. I picked up his trail easy enough, followed it down to L.A., then to Gilmore. I spotted him around the Marker plant the day she blew. I'd spotted all of you, but before I could get there again with Mr. Blake, she blew, everyone scattered. With Walton in jail, Brunner was the one I figured to trace more. I spotted you again at Frieda Brunner's house. I called Mr. Blake here, he said bring you to talk. Here you are."

Blake said, "I want our daughter, Jackson."

"What do you think you can do when you find her?"

Celia Blake said, "Plead with her, try to bring her home, try to make her stay alive, at least."

"That won't be easy," Jackson said. "Not even the last. She doesn't care much for living in this world."

Robert Blake held his fine head. "I'm a rich man, Jackson. I have power, position. Amanda grew up with every advantage. I understand her anguish over this world, I'm not a monster. I know how bad it can be better than she does, or you. I work with men, leaders, who belong in the Middle Ages. I know we have to change, make life more human, more equitable. Real opportunity for everyone, that's the key. No one poor. But we have to advance slowly. Why won't she see that? Why is reform a kind of cowardice to her? To you?"

"Reform never changes the game, Blake, it just smooths the surface, hides the hard core. It's the core your daughter sees as wrong, phony. Your whole view of what life is."

Klegg said, "That sounds like Frank Walton."

"She's Frank Walton's woman, isn't she?" Jackson said.

Robert Blake squeezed his face in his hands. "A man like that! She was always intense, our first child. The boys are good, solid students. They want reform, I've encouraged them. They'll lead us to better things within our values!"

"I can hear Amanda laughing," Jackson said. "Reform in their clean twenty rooms, change in their Cadillacs."

Celia Blake said, "She calls the boys dope peddlars—the opium of reasonable change. The powerful still in power, the poor still safely poor."

"All right, Celia! I know what she thinks!" Robert Blake was up again. "But why? Why?"

"She met Frank Walton," Celia Blake said. "She fell in love. With his image, his reputation, I suppose."

"He took her into S.D.S.," Robert Blake said. "The strikes, the violence. We no longer saw her. Her checks couldn't find her sometimes. We had to let her go, but—"

"She's a woman, Blake, with her own life," Jackson said.

"You—," Robert Blake began, and then walked out of the room.

The father opened the door, walked out into the corridor of the hotel. Jackson watched him, they all did. A Mexican waiter appeared in the hall. Blake didn't even see him. The waiter had to stop for Blake, almost lost his tray, circled around Blake to pass on. Blake never noticed. The Mexican waiter didn't exist for him. Celia Blake saw it all. She sat down, looked up at Jackson.

"She's gone from us, hasn't she, Mr. Jackson? For good. But I can't accept that. She's my child. I want her back."

Robert Blake was back in the room. He closed the door. Jackson sensed the difference in the man. Blake had made his decision. He had been groping, looking for reasons. All that was gone. A moment of question, of doubt, but gone now. A man didn't have Blake's power or money on doubts.

"She'll come back," he said now. "You're one of them, Jackson. Find her for me, you can name your price. You must know ways to find her that we don't. Find her for us, or I'll see you in prison, and I can do it!"

"I believe you," Jackson said. "I'll look for you, but one thing first—did Amanda ever talk about Rosa Brunner? Any trouble she might have had with Rosa Brunner?"

Blake frowned. "Trouble? No, I—"

"Rosa Brunner?" Marty Klegg said, stood away from his wall. "The kid killed in the blast? Why?"

"Rosa Brunner wasn't killed by that blast, Klegg."

Marty Klegg made a noise, looked at Robert Blake. "He's tying your kid to a murder, Mr. Blake! That's what he—"

Robert Blake had a quick mind. Revolution and terrorism was out of his field, but he understood an accusation against one of his family. He barked:

"Klegg, stop—"

Jackson was faster, and this time he didn't make a mistake. His small Mauser was out. Klegg froze. Jackson stepped to the skinny giant, hit him twice. Klegg went down and didn't move.

Jackson backed from the room.

He took the stairs down. Robert Blake wouldn't chase him, and he was in his car and out of the garage without Marty Klegg appearing behind him.

11

It was past midnight when Jackson reached Gilmore again, and the run-down mansion of John Marker. The *santana* wind had gone, a cold desert night wind blowing through the dark streets of the drab city. There were no cars parked around the big house overlooking the railroad yards, but it blazed with light even at the late hour.

John Marker answered the door himself. There were no servants in the mansion, as if John Marker knew he was only passing through. The stocky chemical plant owner was in only his shirt and trousers, his collar open, his thick hair disheveled, his eyes bruised. He seemed to breathe hard.

"He's been here, Marker?" Jackson said. "Adam?"

"Yes, he was here," John Marker said, his eyes filling with a quick anger. "You did it, didn't you? You sent him here! What did you tell him, damn you!"

"Where is he now, Marker?"

"Now? In hell for all I care!"

The businessman turned and walked away down the entry hall of the big house into the bright, warm rear living room with its Italian furniture. Jackson closed the outside door and followed him. Marker lit a cigarette, took a long drink from a tall glass of some straight, dark liquor, stood staring at the empty air. The wife, Christina Marker, stood alone at the far end of the long room, her beautiful face in a kind of pain as she watched her husband. She took no notice of Jackson, her mind on nothing but her husband. Jackson noticed her. He felt her down in his thighs, in his belly. She wore a slim white jersey dress to the floor. It was slit all up one thigh, clung to the full curve of her belly and the hollows of her wide hips.

"I told him that Rosa Brunner was murdered," Jackson said to the businessman. "I told him that maybe that explosion had been no accident, that maybe Rosa Brunner saw someone set it off, that maybe she was killed because she saw. Coming back here was his own idea."

"Murdered?" John Marker said. "No accident?"

"Probably by someone she knew at least a little. You knew her, didn't you? Adam said so. How come you didn't seem to recognize her the night of the explosion?"

"I met her once, a few moments! Months ago. That night I had other things on my mind! My plant, my son missing!"

"And your insurance payoff?"

John Marker seemed to study Jackson for a moment. He smoked, reached down for his glass, took a long drink. He put the glass down carefully as if thinking about something else. He glanced toward his wife.

"Christina, call the police. Now."

Jackson didn't move. He looked at the woman in her slim white dress, then back at John Marker. Marker nodded.

"So, the police don't really worry you," Marker said. "Never mind the police, Christina." The businessman took another drink, his eyes never leaving Jackson's face. "All right, you're no Weatherman, Jackson. What the hell are you? An insurance agent?"

"A private detective working with the Gilmore police on

Rosa Brunner's murder," Jackson said.

"All right, that's better," Marker said. "But you were with that damned terrorist group before it all happened, Adam said so. You were in my plant with them. Why? A police spy?"

"In a way."

Marker nodded again. But there was a certain puzzled look in his eyes, as if for a second other possibilities were occurring to him—maybe even the right possibility. The plant owner had pirated, stolen, from Edgar Callison, and somewhere in his mind he must have considered that Callison might suspect him. Jackson couldn't be sure the thought was in Marker's mind, or how clear it might be, but he moved on quickly to keep the man busy.

"What did Adam want, Marker? What did he do here?"

John Marker drank again, put the glass down. "I don't think he knew what he wanted himself. He's all shaken up. That girl, I suppose. He was always backward with girls; shy and unsure, but with a terrible need. My fault, probably. The father makes the boy a man. In a way he's a good man, morally strong. Wrong, maybe, but honest. Emotionally, he's a boy. Women are too important to him. He smothers a girl."

He drank, wiped his mouth. "He accused me of setting the explosion. He couldn't give me a good reason, and I told him I could prove I was at my health club that night. That stopped him, but it all made me damned angry, and I said his friends probably blew the plant for some damned devious political reason. I told him none of them cared who they killed. He hit me and ran out. That's the last I saw of him."

"Insurance can make a man blow his own plant."

Marker finished his drink. The empty glass had hardly

touched the table before the wife, Christina, was there to take it and refill it from a cognac bottle on a sideboard. She brought it back. John Marker reached up and put his arm around her hips and soft belly. She kissed him, walked back to the far side of the room. Marker watched her, spoke to Jackson.

"What do you know about business, Jackson?"

"Enough."

"Then you should know that the insurance will barely cover the loss, nothing more. It puts me where I started six months ago, except that I've lost those six months, and a year of sales, contracts, prospects, production improvements. I may never be able to start. I'll have to try to find a new plant, and there isn't one in Gilmore. I may not be able to afford a plant somewhere else. The situation here was just right. I'll lose all the staff I had lined up. No, the insurance won't help me beyond breaking even. I'll lose in the end."

Marker picked up his fresh brandy. "Anyway, the company has already paid me in full. Would they do that if they had any suspicions, any reason at all to suspect fraud?"

"Maybe they don't know enough. That bomb group makes a very good cover," Jackson said. "Maybe no one knows enough, Marker. Maybe you needed cash more than a business. Have you been married long?"

"Three years, damn it! Leave my marriage out of this. If you're looking at this house, we're just renting, why bother with it? My home is in Los Angeles. Gilmore had a cheap plant I could use. If it had gotten going, we would have moved back to L.A. We will now, anyway."

Jackson nodded slowly. "All right. Did Adam kill Rosa Brunner, Marker? You say he's sexually unstable. Jealous?"

"I don't know," the father said. "Something happened

to Adam in prison. Not just the usual bitterness, not just anger at being put in jail for his principles. Something more basic, almost a personality change. He was an open boy; too honest, too ready to tell you what he thought. He lived here with us briefly when he came home. He hardly ever spoke. He brought that Rosa around once, and her father once. He never told me anything about them, and he moved out very soon. I never had the faintest suspicion of what he was doing. Nothing! Making bombs in my own plant, and I never had a hint. That's what scares me most —they mean business, don't they? They're not playing a game, these terrorist kids. If Adam could change that much, from open to all hidden, from pacifist to bomb-maker, what else could he do?"

John Marker breathed hard in the room as if he had been running a long distance. In a way he had—running back through the life of his son.

"Did Adam say anything this time, tonight, that gave any hint he might have killed the girl?"

"No. He couldn't have killed her, Jackson. I know that." The businessman said it, but he didn't know. He drank, a long drink, held the glass in both hands. "What's happened to this country, Jackson? Where did the dreams go, the ideals? A man getting all he wanted by his own efforts? Hard work and the good life? Fair play for everyone, a government for the people? Opportunity to go as far as you wanted?"

"Did it ever exist, Marker? Did any of us ever work only by our own efforts, rise without using others? Was it ever fair, or was it rigged to favor special groups? Did everyone have opportunity, was the government for all people? Was the dream an abstraction no one ever really wanted, or con job by those on top who always knew better?

'The kids in Weatherman say that."

"Then they'll destroy the whole country!"

"That's what they want to do."

"What's wrong with them, damn it? Why can't they want what most men want? Success. Something more for themselves!"

"Idealism," Jackson said. "And guilt, too. Our guilt."

John Marker was silent. He didn't even take a drink this time. He got up, but he didn't pace. He stood there like a man in some wilderness trying to see through the trees.

"You know the *Rubaiyat*, Jackson?"

"I've read it."

> "Ah, take the Cash, and let the Credit go,
> Nor heed the rumble of a distant Drum!"

Marker seemed to listen to his words himself, still trying to see through a forest he didn't understand. "I tried to teach Adam, but he went his own way. All of them. They'll kill for that distant drum, and die for it."

"Where could Adam go, Marker?"

"I don't know, and that's the truth." The businessman sat down again. "I could say I don't care, too. I've said it, haven't I? But that's not quite the truth, is it?"

John Marker took another drink, smiled. The wife, Christina, came to Marker as Jackson went out. She held Marker's arm.

In his car, Jackson drove to a telephone and called the Gilmore police headquarters. Sergeant Prather had nothing to report, except that Frank Walton might get bail soon.

Time was closing in.

Jackson got onto the freeway and drove fast west toward Los Angeles. Even the great, hungry city was quiet and still when he turned off the freeway into North Hollywood. He was fighting sleep. He had driven a lot of miles, done a lot of work, since that morning in Santa Barbara. Too many miles.

Number 142 Ensenada Court was dark and deserted. He got out of his car and walked up the walk beside the burned-out center grass of the court. There was still no light in Gerhard Myers' cottage. Jackson rang. No answer. He tried the door again. It was still unlocked.

Inside he went through the two rooms. No one was there. The bathroom window where Adam Marker had climbed out was still open. No one was here, and Jackson didn't think anyone had been here. Maybe no one ever would be. At least, not Gerhard Myers.

He'd think about it tomorrow. He had to sleep.

He drove to the first motel he could find with a vacancy sign. He carried his bags into the unit, and lay down without undressing. He was asleep in two minutes.

12

It was almost 10 A.M. when Jackson woke. He cursed himself for oversleeping. He was showered and dressed in ten minutes, and out to his car with his bags. He stopped only long enough for a bowl of cereal and coffee. Then he drove back to 142 Ensenada Court.

A little, round-faced, balding man with a small belly and wrinkled, sun-browned skin sat in a deck chair in front of Gerhard Myers' cottage. Wisps of stiff, white hair ringed his skull. He wore only a pair of bathing trunks, and his eyes were closed as he lay in the warm sun. About sixty-five, he looked like a million shoe clerks and office workers—except for two deep scars on his face and chest—bullet scars.

"Gerhard Myers?" Jackson said.

"No," the little man said. He didn't open his eyes. "What do you want? Leave me alone. Go away."

The short sentences came out in jagged spurts as if Myers were answering questions only he had asked.

"I want Emil Brunner," Jackson said.

"Go away. Gerhard Myers is dead."

But the little man opened his eyes. They were brown and gentle, a sharp contrast to the bullet scars. Myers seemed to listen to the morning, his round head cocked as if hearing footsteps. He was—footsteps echoing down silent corridors of the past he wanted to forget, the violent corridors of bullets he was trying to forget.

"I don't know Emil Brunner."

"His wife says you do."

"Once I knew Emil Brunner. No more. Frieda is wrong."

Jackson lit one of his thin cigars. "Scared, Myers?"

"Scared? Yes, always," the little man said. He looked at Jackson. "You always come. You smoke cigars and ask the questions that don't matter because you know the answers before you come. Police. The other side. What does it matter?"

"I'm not the police," Jackson said.

"Always we fail," Gerhard Myers said. "No one cares. No one wants us to succeed. The people do not want us to win, they do not want to change, they do not know that anything is wrong to be changed. They like their cage. They do not thank us for telling them they are in a cage. I have failed in ten countries. We all have. In Spain we failed large, here we failed small. In Cuba we won, but I was not there, and did we really win? Who knows? And always you come."

"I'm not an enemy, Myers."

"Enemies come, friends come. What is the difference?"

"You're scared of friends, too?"

"Today's friend is tomorrow's enemy. The shifts of wind. A revolutionist lives without place, status, role or even real name in the day-to-day world. What he does is only disguise. His life is his cause, his place is the movement, his roots are his theory. He must fight for this theory to the last comma. The slightest deviation is disaster, changes brother to enemy. A difference of opinion is a cataclysm. Forty years I worked for a vision of justice, peace, equality and humanity. No more. There is no hope for mankind. An animal who only wants to be master for the moment. I am tired. I want peace and silence. I want to sit in the sun like Lazarus."

The old revolutionary closed his eyes again. Jackson smoked and looked around the shabby court. He wondered how many such places Gerhard Myers had lived in. Out of a suitcase with a single change of clothes. The price a man paid for rejecting what the world told him he could have. Now he wanted only here and the sun.

"Wash your hands, Myers?" Jackson said. "You can't do it. No one can let you. I can't. Did Emil Brunner come to you?"

"No."

"I can go, but others will come. The police. I want to help Brunner. I don't know what the police would do."

Myers opened his eyes. "He came to me. I told him I had no help for him. I took a message to Frieda. Emil went, that is all." The scarred little man turned his eyes up to Jackson. "I helped them raise Rosa. City to city, room to room. I loved her. A revolutionist should not have children. His life is lived for the children of others, he has nothing left for his own child. He came here, Emil, running. His daughter was dead, but that was not what he thought about, no! He came to me to escape, to go on with the cause. His child is dead, but he does not think of that. He cannot go to the funeral—some plan for the cause that he must work on, that excites him! Always the Cause, and I am finished. No more. I will mourn the dead. I will mourn for Rosa, I will not think again of Emil Brunner!"

"Emil has some plan? Some scheme for the movement?"

"His daughter lies dead from some mistake, and he is eager! He knows something that will help the Cause. I told Frieda what Emil does, and what I feel. I will sit here in the sun. I will not think of mankind anymore. I think we are a mistake, we humans. A mistake of nature. Something went wrong in our evolution, something is missing in us. A mistake."

"Mistake or not, we're here. We have to go on, and no one can escape what he is, what he's done."

"I can," Gerhard Myers said. "There are no charges against me. I am not a fugitive. All my sentences have been served. I will rest. No more dreams, no more fears."

"You said you loved Rosa Brunner," Jackson said. "She didn't die by accident, Myers. She was murdered—before the explosion."

Myers sat up. "Murdered? Rosa?"

"It's possible the explosion was rigged. You say Emil has some plan, maybe he knows who killed Rosa. If he does, then he could be in big danger."

"Murdered?" Gerhard Myers said. "And Emil could—?"

The struggle on the little man's face was agonizing to watch. The human struggle, in a way—reason against hope; need for self, against need to serve; reality against dream. It is there somewhere in every man—the need to serve as well as to serve yourself. Meyers fought a battle between his decision of today, and his loyalties of yesterday.

"When he left here he said he would go to a place where he would be safe and still close," Gerhard Myers said. "To a hostel for street people, an old comrade, Peter Matchka. It is in Isla Vista. That is—"

"I know where it is," Jackson said. "Thanks, Myers."

"Mistake, all of us," the little man said. "Illusion, and there is no escape."

The last Jackson saw of Gerhard Myers, he was lying back in his deck chair in the sun, but his eyes were not closed. Eyes of defeat, as if he knew that even the sun would not help him.

Jackson drove north. He didn't like it. Santa Barbara was his home, he could be seen by people he did not want to see him at work. But it was a chance he had to take.

There was no way to know how soon Frank Walton would be free on bail. Once free, Walton would sooner or later guess what Jackson was doing. The murder of Rosa Brunner, the capture of her killer, would be unimportant compared to closing ranks against an outsider spying among them.

Unless Frank Walton had killed her—and that would make it worse.

He passed around Santa Barbara after lunch, went off the freeway at Los Carneros Road, and turned right into the university town of Isla Vista. The few students strolled idly in the autumn sun, lay on the grass, sat on the balconies and steps of the handsome-looking modern apartments built of plywood and chicken wire and overcharged by landlords who cried loudly over the immorality of the young. The same landlords who complained of marijuana and whisky, and fought in Sacramento to have beer and booze legalized in Isla Vista so they could sell it.

The street hostel was an apartment complex with a sign over the door. Five street people, men and women, were working on the grounds. A truck loaded with rakes and tools for street cleanup was parked in front, with four bearded men waiting in it. Jackson went up the walk. The street people watched him warily. They had a sixth sense for authorities. They had learned they needed it to survive.

Inside, Jackson found the office of the Director. He went

in and sat down. The man behind the desk looked up at him.

"Hello, Pete," Jackson said.

Peter Matchka was a slender man of fifty, bald and bearded, sun and wind burned, two fingers missing on his left hand.

"What is it, Kane?" the hostel director said.

"I'm looking for Emil Brunner."

Matchka went back to his work. "I'm out of touch."

"No you're not," Jackson said. "He's hot, blew up down south in Gilmore. Gerhard Myers says he came to you. Gerhard wants to wash his hands of it. He can't. Neither can you."

Peter Matchka leaned back. "I run a hostel. It's good work. We walk a thin line. The community hates the kids for wandering, the radicals hate the kids for not joining a group. Nobody wants the kids to live how they want. We do. I'm not going to hurt our work because my past gets dragged up to scare the good citizens or give the militants a hold on me."

"From revolution to community welfare? No more utopia?"

"Maybe utopia is inside."

"If Marx had lived long enough maybe he'd have run a soup kitchen. Emil Brunner hasn't given up utopia, though, he's still fighting, and I want him."

Peter Matchka got up and went to his window. Two street people were busily digging weeds outside. "They're human beings, Kane. Good ones, making their own better world. No one wants to let them. One side wants them kicked on and on, the other side wants them to accept some narrow program."

"They're in trouble. They won't believe. That hurts."

"They're happy here," Matchka said. "They have food, a place to sleep, and they want to work for it. They don't have to take speed or acid to keep awake all night and not get hassled by the police. Until we opened up they had to steal to eat, break into empty apartments to sleep, commandeer community rooms for shelter. Since we took over, burglaries are way down, trespassing is almost gone, no riots, no destruction of property, a lot less drugs. It works, Kane."

"As long as the militants let it, as long as the community doesn't try to preach or meddle."

"They've got the strength to resist now. All they want is to be left alone, but everyone needs support to fight. They don't carry weapons anymore, and they do good work. Let me alone, Kane. Go away."

"I can't, Pete."

"A break?"

"No, Pete, sorry."

"All right. You want something, I'll sell it at a price."

"What price?"

"You leave me alone from here on in."

"If I can. Where is Emil? How about the others?"

"Others?"

"Adam Marker and Amanda Blake."

"I don't know them. I just couldn't turn Emil away. I sent him through Weatherman channels. Way underground, you understand? Emil didn't know the contact here."

"Who is the contact?"

"You don't know?" Matchka said. He sat down behind his battered old desk. "You're a smooth one, Kane. A big front in the Establishment here, and perfect credentials in Weatherman. Lots of money, but I don't really know where it comes from, do I? It's the best Establishment cover I ever saw, or the best fake underground record. I wonder which?"

"Which do you think, Pete?" Jackson said.

"Maybe both," Matchka said. "All sides against the middle. Kane Jackson for himself. Double agent? Triple? Everything is a cover for Kane Jackson?"

"Sounds like fun," Jackson said. "Have you passed that idea around much?"

"No, and I won't. You people fight your wars, I'll feed the casualties. I don't care what you are, or who pays you. You want to find Emil Brunner, go to Pat Stanley, 2050 Anacapa Street in Santa Barbara. Don't say I sent you."

"I tailed Brunner," Jackson said.

As he went out, Jackson saw the two street people laughing in the sun. The man was bare to the waist as he worked. He stopped to kiss the girl. She rubbed his bare chest, slowly, as if wondering what beautiful things he was made of.

13

The Anacapa Street address was on the Upper East Side of Santa Barbara, an area of big houses that had once been the richest section. It still was in many places, and the quiet, gardened streets were a sharp contrast to the jerry-built glitter of Isla Vista. There were smaller houses now, the old estates cut up and sold in pieces, and many of the big mansions were run-down. They were bought by middle-class people who wanted space and good schools but didn't have a lot of money, and by the commune people.

Number 2050 was a two-story pink stucco monster of some twenty rooms set in half an acre of ground now overgrown with weeds. Five battered cars were parked in the neglected driveway, a pickup truck was on what had been the lawn. Two men in face hair and overalls, and two women in long dresses, sat on the overgrown lawn. They watched Jackson park and come up the brick walk.

He nodded to them. They didn't nod back. Two small girls ran up from somewhere and stood close to the adults. The whole group watched him with suspicion, wary. They had lived their brief lives with trouble that always came from the outside, from men in fatigues as well as men in good business suits. They had been hurt too often by strangers—different kinds of victims of Establishment and of militants. As Jackson went up the stairs into the house, he saw the four adults gather up the children and climb into the pickup truck. They had learned the lesson of today well—don't be involved, run.

Inside the big house he found the name of Patricia Stanley on one of a series of mailboxes that had been added to the wall just inside the front door. So Pat Stanley was a woman. It didn't surprise him, the rage of their women was the deadliest weapon of Weatherman. Her room was 2-D. Jackson went up an elegant curved staircase that had once been soft, dark wood but needed refinishing. He knocked at the right rear door at the end of the second floor hall. A woman answered.

"Come in."

Jackson went into a sunny room that was sparsely furnished with secondhand pieces, and littered with books and papers. A tall, slender, dark-haired woman sat at a desk working over a thick manuscript. She didn't turn around or get up. Jackson heard movement and sounds he couldn't place. They seemed to come from behind a screen in a corner away from the windows.

"Miss Stanley?" Jackson said.

The woman turned. She stood up abruptly. "What are you doing here?"

Jackson leaned against a table. "They're looking for me, too. How many names do you have, Amanda?"

Amanda Blake went to the door, looked out. She came back to face Jackson. In the black wig her whole face seemed different. She wore a very proper, reserved dress.

"Were you followed?"

"No," Jackson said.

"You're sure?"

"As sure as I can be. I know my work, Amanda."

The tall girl seemed to think about that. The noises from behind the screen became louder. Amanda Blake went behind the screen, came back out carrying an infant in diapers. The sounds of the baby hadn't clicked in Jackson's brain, he hadn't been considering the possibility of a baby here. Amanda Blake soothed the infant against her breast, calmed it.

"Why did you come to me?" she said to Jackson.

"I didn't. I was sent to Pat Stanley. I'm looking for Emil Brunner."

"Sent?" Amanda Blake nodded. "Matchka. Of course. No hope for those old-line movement people. Pacifists, Stalinists, civil-righters, ban-the-bomb boobs. They call us adventurists, oppose us all the way. It won't work, they say. Talk, talk. Talk is what the fascists want. They set the rules, and as long as we talk nothing will happen. Emil had to go to Matchka. When they're in trouble they run to their old friends like dogs—help me, old comrade!"

The baby squirmed and began to cry against her breast. She sat down in an easy chair. She whispered softly to the infant, a small smile on her face for the child, her eyes still cold as she thought about all those who didn't think as she did.

"How long have you been Pat Stanley?" Jackson asked.

"Two years. It's useful. Pat Stanley is a good, solid doctoral candidate at the University. Working on her dissertation on the customs of the Hopi Indians. All legitimate. I've got a solid identity here, good cover for Amanda Blake. Frank Walton taught me how. He uses three identities you can trace all day and never suspect. Besides, Pat Stanley is real, too. I want the doctorate, the solid place, the spotless reputation. That way, I can do a lot more damage."

"That's why your parents can't contact you half the time? They don't know Pat Stanley."

"My parents? What do you know about them? How?"

"You didn't know that they're here in California, in Gilmore and L.A., looking for you? They even hired a detective."

She didn't answer at once. The baby had begun to cry hard. She unbuttoned her blouse-dress, unhooked her nursing brassiere, began to feed the baby from her swollen left breast. The child sucked happily, making small sounds.

"Where did you have the baby in Gilmore?" Jackson said.

"With me," she said. "Not where we made the bombs."

"That's why you left sometimes, to feed it."

"Yes," she said, but her voice wasn't interested now in the child. She seemed unaware of the child or of her bare breast, a part of her. "So they *are* here."

"You thought they could be?"

She gently stroked the child at her breast, but didn't look down at it. "They sent me to boarding school, then to Smith. They sent me to Europe in my junior year. To study art. When I graduated and wanted to help in the Peace Corps, they encouraged me. Such good people, yes. I went to Bolivia to help the Indians. Two years. But I didn't help, no. The suffering and the poverty didn't go away. They didn't need help or handouts, they needed the end of the world of my good parents! Nothing else would help them. Only the end of white America! Our world of privilege that enslaves men without them even knowing it. We're not an oppressive society, police and all that. We're a repressive society—we repress all in men that's really human, free. We repress all humanity, make men think they want their chains!"

"You met your parents in Gilmore, Amanda?"

"No," the girl snapped. She shifted the baby at her breast, soothed it gently. "Why do you want to find Emil? The group blew up with those bombs. It's finished."

"It left a loose end."

"Loose end?"

"Rosa Brunner."

"People have to die sometimes to win."

"Do people have to be murdered?"

She removed the infant from her breast, settled the breast more comfortably, put the eager child back. With one hand she found a cigarette on a table, lit it with a solid gold lighter monogrammed: A.B. The privilege of her past pursued her in a hundred subtle, unconscious ways. The tailored jeans in Gilmore, the gold lighter, the checks she used to buy dynamite. She could destroy her privilege, but she couldn't escape it.

"Was Rosa murdered, Jackson?" she said as she smoked.

"Didn't you know already?"

"No."

"From Emil Brunner if no other way? He knows, doesn't he?"

"He didn't tell me," she said. "Why are you so worried about it? What is a murder to you?"

"It's a killer inside the movement, Amanda."

"You think it was one of us?"

"Unless someone else was there that night. Do you know if anyone else could have been there?"

"The plant exploded, Rosa died, that's all I know."

"You're sure, Amanda?"

"Yes."

"No," Jackson said. "You saw your parents in Gilmore, didn't you? At least your father. You must have seen him near the plant that night. You knew they were in Gilmore. They'd do almost anything to save you from yourself, wouldn't they? Even blow up the bombs."

She nodded slowly, touched her feeding child. "Yes, I saw him. My father. I thought I might have, I wasn't sure. Near the plant in the dark when I came back from feeding the baby that night. I thought I'd made a mistake. But, yes, I think my father would do anything he thought he had to for me."

"Was anyone around when you ran out with Adam Marker?"

"No."

"Does Emil Brunner know your father? Did Rosa?"

"Not that I know."

"Emil ran out of the plant first. He has some plan, probably to get money for the movement. That's what would matter to him. Did he see someone in the plant, run out first to try to catch the person?"

"I don't know. Emil told me nothing."

Jackson watched her. The child had stopped eating, was going to sleep. Amanda Blake stood up and carried the baby behind the screen again. Jackson heard her humming quietly to the child. When she came out, her dress was buttoned.

"Is the baby part of your cover?" Jackson said.

"Women have babies."

"And husbands?"

"Why? Is a husband important?"

"No husband, but a baby has a father."

"Usually."

"Frank Walton?"

"I know who the father is, no one else needs to."

"I need to," Jackson said. "Rosa Brunner was in love with Walton. What did Frank Walton think about that?"

"I couldn't say."

"You didn't like Rosa much, did you? You don't seem too sorry she's dead."

"I didn't like her, I'm not sorry she's dead," Amanda Blake said. "But not because of sex, or love, whatever you want to call it. She was a weak link, a bad revolutionary. She wasn't hard enough, she made mistakes. Perhaps that's what went wrong and blew up."

"Drugs?"

"Frank thought so. Perhaps Emil did too."

"Dangerous. His own daughter. But he might do it, yes?"

"He might. Sometimes he had the guts."

"You too. You have guts, right? Kill a danger?"

"That's more possible than love, but I didn't kill anyone."

"Then there's Adam Marker. He was hung up on Rosa."

She laughed suddenly, a strange sound from her. "And if he was my baby's father, then I killed her to keep Adam! Why not Emil? Maybe he was the father?"

"Someone murdered Rosa," Jackson said.

"Then find out who, Jackson. If it worries you."

"Where do I find Emil Brunner now, Amanda?"

"A cabin up on Mountain Drive, 1640. If he's there."

"Alone?"

"As far as I know."

"You haven't seen Adam Marker?"

"No."

"When does Frank Walton get out of jail on bail?"

"I don't know. Maybe never. Accidents happen in jail."

"Yes, they do," Jackson said. "You know, it's odd, you say the group is finished, but none of you have run very far. I wonder why? As if you're all waiting for something. Or maybe the group isn't finished?"

Amanda Blake only shrugged. No one was going to learn much from her. She was a tougher revolutionary than anyone.

14

The movement caught Jackson's eye as he walked down the steps of the pink house. A flash of something dark behind a hedge across the street. He didn't break his stride, reached his car, got in, and drove away. At Mission Street he turned right, circled three blocks, and came back toward the pink house from the opposite direction.

The Ford was parked around the corner from where Amanda Blake lived, and a block away. The skinny man's Ford, Marty Klegg. Jackson drove to the alley behind the pink house, and parked. He took a thin nylon rope from his equipment case, and a small steel grappling hook. He climbed a fence to the rear of the pink house. He threw the hook up to the parapet of the flat roof. It caught the first time, and he went up the rope fast and silent. He swung lightly to just below Amanda Blake's window, looked in cautiously. With luck he might hear some interesting conversation.

He didn't. Amanda Blake sat alone at her desk working on her dissertation. No one else was in the room. The tall girl was unaware of Jackson outside her window. He made a fixed loop in his nylon cord for his foot, rested hanging with one eye looking into the room, and waited. Ten minutes passed. No one saw him hanging there on the face of the building. Then Amanda Blake looked up from her work—but not at the window.

The tall girl raised her head and looked toward her door. She got up and went to the door, looked out. Jackson watched her listen, come back into the room, close the door, and go to a chest of drawers. She moved quickly, sharply, like a man. She stood behind her door. After a moment, the door opened and Marty Klegg pushed it all the way open and stepped into the room. He came in three full steps. That was his mistake.

Amanda Blake stepped out behind him. She had a long police billy club. She knew how to use it, hit Klegg twice on the side of the head. The skinny giant went down sprawled on his face. Amanda Blake moved like an athlete, was on the fallen Klegg with a rope in her hands. She hogtied his hands and feet together behind his back like a champion cowboy tying a calf. Klegg was already moving, groaning on the floor, helpless. The tall girl didn't even look at him again.

She went behind the screen, came out carrying her baby in a harness on her back, and walked out of the room. She took nothing but her child with her. She would have other rooms to go to. Jackson hung outside the window for a few more minutes. The tall girl did not come back. Jackson pulled himself up to the window, opened it, swung inside. On the floor Marty Klegg was swearing. Jackson squatted in front of the helpless man.

"Well, you found her, Klegg," he said. "Now what?"

"You going to cut me loose, or play games?"

"I'm not sure yet. Is Blake around?"

"He's around."

"You think he'd like to talk to me again?"

"No."

"She got away, maybe I know where."

"Blake'll talk then."

"Good. A friendly talk, right?" He searched Klegg, took his big pistol from the shoulder holster, and the small gun from a belt holster Klegg wore on the small of his back. "Just to be sure it's a friendly talk."

"How about your gun?" Klegg said, his face on the floor.

"I know I'm friendly," Jackson said.

He took his pocket knife out, cut the ropes. Marty Klegg sat up, cursed, rubbed his ankles, and uncoiled like a snake to his feet. He looked around the room as if he had to do something positive.

"My car's in the alley," Jackson said. "Go wait in yours, I'll follow you."

"You figure I won't skip?"

"I've got things Blake wants to hear. And I've got your guns, right?"

Klegg shrugged, walked from the room. Jackson went down and around to the rear of the pink house. He retrieved his rope and hook, carried them to his car, put them back into his equipment case, and drove around the block to Klegg's Ford. The skinny man drove to State Street, turned east. He led Jackson to the Pepper Tree Motel on upper State. They went up to the second floor balcony of the third unit. Klegg knocked. Robert Blake opened the door, Jackson pushed Klegg inside and went in closing the door behind him.

"Klegg, what the devil—" Robert Blake began.

"We decided on a conference," Jackson said.

Klegg said, "I found her, lost her, and Jackson says he maybe knows where she's gone."

Klegg leaned against a wall again. It was the skinny man's height, only leaning was really comfortable. Klegg lit a cigarette. He hadn't said how he had lost Amanda Blake, and Jackson didn't expose him—professional courtesy. Robert Blake stood in the center of the motel room, his Yaleman face pale and waiting. The mother, Celia Blake, was at the window again, as if she spent her whole life looking out windows for her lost child to come home. She wore tailored slacks and an orange shirt, and looked ten years younger, trim and tailored.

"Well?" Robert Blake licked at his lips. "Where is she?"

"Later," Jackson said. He stood with his back against the door, casually, but where he could see them all, and no one could get behind him. "It won't do you any good to find her, you know that, don't you?"

"Just tell us where to find her," Blake said, his imposing face reddening. "I'll handle the rest."

"Money? Don't even try. You don't have a prayer of reaching her anyway, but money is the last way. She'd take it and skip and buy bombs. She's a grown woman, Blake, and she's made her choice. Final. She means it as much as anyone I ever met. You don't even live in the world with her now, believe me."

Klegg nodded at his wall. "Jackson's right, Mr. Blake. I've been digging, she's a solid leftie all the way. Real hardcore. I know, I've seen enough of them. No way."

"I don't give a damn what you know," Robert Blake said. "I don't care what you think, either of you. I—"

The mother, Celia Blake, made a sudden sound, almost a moan. They all looked at her. She stood staring out her window. Her voice seemed to come from somewhere else, another time:

"She was just a happy girl, so happy. At school, at Smith. A gentle girl who only wanted good for others. We visited her down there in Bolivia. She was happy helping those miserable Indians, easing their misery. She changed . . . changed—"

Robert Blake swore, clenched his fists. "That damned bastard Frank Walton! He—"

"Only partly," Jackson said. "Those Indians she wanted to help in Bolivia. What she found out was that those Indians couldn't be helped, not by handouts or all the good will in the world. She worked for two years to make their suffering go away, but the poverty and suffering didn't go away. You educated her to think, so she did. You raised her to be a winner, to come out on top, to do things fast and hard, and that's how she has to act—no compromise."

"What did we ever do but love her, give her everything?" Robert Blake cried. "When she went to jail, we even bailed her out, came to her help! Even when she spat at us we—"

"Worst thing you could have done," Jackson snapped. "To her you gave her a sick world, and she felt with the victims. She wanted to be a victim, and you were a mover of the world she hated. She convicts *you* of Viet Nam, Laos, Bolivia, Cuba, the Dominican, Appalachia, Oakland!"

"What did I have to do with any of that? No, I—"

"You made what led to all that, in her eyes, Blake. You got rich from what led to all that. We all did—to her."

"What does she want, my blood?"

"Yes, that's just what she wants."

In the silence that settled over the motel room, even Marty Klegg seemed to be looking inside, thinking. How did any of them understand Amanda Blake? She could not understand them. Long ago decisions had been made by people none of them had ever met or heard of, the world had been sent down a road that led, inevitably, to both Robert Blake and Amanda. From the first man who bought tools instead of inheriting them, and hired another man who had no tools to work for him, both Robert Blake and

Amanda had come into existence, the lines drawn. One man had the power of money, and another had only his work to sell, and two different worlds were born. They led to Blake and John Marker, and to Amanda and Emil Brunner, and somewhere in the middle Rosa Brunner had died.

Jackson said, "You know Amanda has a baby?"

"Baby?" Robert Blake said. "She's married? To who? That damned—"

"No, she's not married. I don't know who the father is."

Celia Blake seemed to shiver at her window. "She turned her back on all we believe, didn't she? Is it a boy?"

"I don't know. I don't know who the father is, but I want to know. Rosa Brunner was in love with Frank Walton. Adam Marker loved Rosa. Did Amanda ever mention Adam Marker?"

"No!" Robert Blake snapped. "My daughter may want my blood, but she's no murderer!"

"Maybe not," Jackson said. "Is Emil Brunner blackmailing you, Blake? Asking for money?"

The imposing industrialist blinked at Jackson, his mouth open. Celia Blake turned from her window. Marty Klegg was studying Jackson now, his small eyes very bright and alert, something happening in the skinny man's sharp eyes, a kind of question and answer at the same time. Robert Blake appeared to be puzzled, yet cautious.

"Brunner? That girl's father? No, why would he? You're still trying to prove that Amanda killed that girl?"

Jackson said, "You told me you traced Frank Walton to Gilmore, found us all at the Marker Chemical plant the day it blew up. You said Klegg there found us, reported back to you, Blake, but the plant exploded before you could get to Amanda. That means you were there, in Gilmore, at the plant or near, the night of the explosion. Not just Klegg, but you too, Blake."

Robert Blake licked his lips. "No, we didn't get there in time. That plant had—"

"She saw you, Blake. Amanda saw you," Jackson said.

The industrialist was silent. He looked at Marty Klegg. Celia Blake had sat down now, she held onto the arms of the chair. Marty Klegg leaned back against his wall.

"You know, Jackson," Klegg said, "you're kind of a funny Weatherman. Not like most of them I know. Too smooth, too slick, you've been around and you work real well on this kind of detective work. I can smell something phony. You're just not like the rest, and ever since that plant blew up you've been acting awful funny. Like a man with a job, you know? Not a job for Weatherman, but maybe against."

"I have a job—to find a murderer, Klegg."

"For the movement? No, there's something else. A cop?"

"I'm no cop," Jackson said.

"No," Klegg agreed, "not a cop. Not Weatherman, either. But you were there, with them. I wonder why? You're a pro, I can tell a pro. What was a professional snooper doing in that group? Spying? Or maybe something else, you were out of the place before it blew. And why the big snooping now?"

"Think about it," Jackson said. "Think about Amanda seeing Blake at that plant just before it exploded. Maybe Blake wanted to do more than just talk Amanda out of what she was doing. Some action to get rid of a bomb factory, a Weatherman group."

"With my daughter inside, Jackson?" Robert Blake said.

"She wasn't hurt. Klegg's a professional, too. An explosion can be rigged to make sure no one is hurt."

"Rosa Brunner was hurt," Robert Blake said.

"Not by the explosion. Did she see you, Blake? Or maybe

it was Klegg she saw?"

Marty Klegg said, "You've got a nasty mind, Jackson."

"You were both there. You found her earlier that day, Klegg. Then you say you just took too long, got back to the plant too late to reach Amanda. I'd have thought you'd have reported in an instant, Klegg, and Blake would have come running fast to his daughter. What took so long?"

"I had to think, decide how to talk to her," Robert Blake said. "I delayed. We got there before it blew up, yes, but only by perhaps an hour. I met Klegg there, and—"

"You *met* Klegg there? The two of you didn't go to the Marker plant together?"

Klegg looked at Robert Blake. Blake cleared his throat.

"No, we met there," the industrialist said.

Jackson's voice was quiet. "So you could have been there before Klegg without him knowing it?"

Marty Klegg said, "Don't say anything more, Mr. Blake."

"You'd do anything to break Amanda loose from Weatherman, wouldn't you?" Jackson said. "Try anything. Money, power, talk, cheating, even blow up a plant? Even murder?"

Marty Klegg said, "Find some proof, Jackson. You do that, and I'm going to find out about you. You were there too."

"I was there," Jackson said. "But I don't have a daughter whose life I want to live for her. Blake does. I wonder how hard he'd try to shape her life for her? Blake's a man who gets things done, has power and uses it. Only maybe someone saw him use it that night. If Emil Brunner saw you, Blake, you'll pay the rest of your life. Unless you tell what happened."

"No one saw me," Robert Blake said. "There was nothing to see, nothing to tell. All I want is my daughter. Tell me where she is now, Jackson."

"I don't know," Jackson said. "Sorry, I had to talk to you. You'll have to find her again yourself. If you really want to, if it isn't Emil Brunner you really want."

Robert Blake's hands clenched as if he wished he had them around Jackson's throat. Marty Klegg was only thoughtful. Celia Blake didn't even move as Jackson walked out of the motel room. She looked like a woman who knows hope is gone.

15

The cabin on Mountain Drive was down a steep dirt drive at the bottom of an overgrown *barranca*. Only the roof and front were visible in the early evening sunlight. There was no car parked at the cabin. Jackson coasted down the drive, the crunch of his wheels in gravel the only sound except the mockingbirds in the thick trees and brush.

Jackson got out of his car, swore softly to himself. Amanda Blake had said—*if* Brunner was at the cabin. It was beginning to look like Emil Brunner was keeping just one jump ahead of Jackson, as if, somehow, Brunner was aware of every move Jackson made. Aware, and wary, because he had some scheme for the movement, the Cause. A scheme that could only mean one of two things—money or pressure.

The glint in the evening sun came from the low porch at the front of the cabin. Something lodged between two boards of the porch. Jackson walked up on the low porch, bent to inspect the glinting.

It looked like a coin, silver, the size of a silver half dollar. He reached and pried it from the crack between the boards. It wasn't a coin.

A small silver medal with a loop at the top and a relief engraving on the side Jackson looked at. The engraving was a sailboat with a single mast, the boat sailing on silver waves with mountains in the background. Jackson turned it over. The script engraving on the reverse side read: *Star Class, Adam Marker, 7-4-65.*

Jackson remained squatting on the porch in the evening sun as he looked at the medal. It was heavily scratched, as if carried for some time with other hard objects rubbing against it. On a key chain, probably, in a pocket with coins and other metal objects since 1965.

Jackson stood up, looked at the closed door of the cabin. He tried the knob. It was unlocked. He went inside.

Emil Brunner lay sprawled on a couch on the far side of the bare, rustic living room. The low sun streamed in through a wide picture window that made up the whole rear wall of the cabin and had a view of the whole coast and the sea beyond.

Blood had formed in a pool under the couch, was still red and liquid. Emil Brunner had not been dead long.

Jackson didn't have to go any closer to know that Emil Brunner was dead. The chest was a mass of blood from at least three separate bullet wounds. A fourth wound in the head had bled down over his face. One shot had missed, left a torn scar in the wall over the couch.

But not more than an hour, probably less, the blood wet, and the smell of exploded powder heavy and acrid in the room.

Jackson walked stiffly, the presence of death affecting his legs as it still did, always. He bent down over the dead revolutionary. Closer, he could see the four bullet wounds through the blood. Smallish wounds, but in the brain and heart, Brunner must have been dead before he slumped back on the couch. Jackson raised the body to look under. None of the bullets had come out. A small caliber gun, no more than 7.65 mm, probably less—a .25 or even a .22 caliber.

Five shots—a fusillade.

Jackson stood and looked all around the cabin room. It was a living room, neat and clean and almost bare—a place to come for weekends, perhaps. It was all in order, as if cleaned and set in order when someone left, and he saw nothing that could have belonged to Emil Brunner.

The kitchen had been used, the remains of a meal of canned beans and some frozen meat on the kitchen table. A pot of coffee was still warm on the gas stove. The refrigerator was scrubbed, held a quart of milk, some eggs, and a loaf of white bread and some butter. The freezer compartment contained two TV dinners, salisbury steak, and three frozen packaged meats. All the food of a man in a temporary stay.

The bedroom had been slept in, the bed still unmade. A suitcase was open on the floor. It held a change of clothes, extra shoes, some candy, a heavy army .38 caliber pistol, loaded, a box of ammunition, and a large notebook. In the notebook were pages of what appeared to be names and addresses, but all in an obvious code. There were other pages of drawings, notes on organizations and weapons, and a final section of day-to-day memoranda. The last entry in the day-to-day section was for yesterday: *Channel Marina, Oxnard Shores, all meet*. None of the earlier entries for a month told Jackson anything.

In the living room again, Jackson searched the body. He found keys, five dollars in bills and change, and a wallet with credit cards in many names, and three pictures of a little girl—Rosa Brunner as a child. The Cause may have been all to Emil Brunner, but maybe not quite all. He had not been oblivious to his daughter, no. If he had chased whatever his scheme had been so hard, it had been to go on, to avenge a daughter who was dead and could not be helped anymore.

Jackson stood up. He looked down at Emil Brunner. Somehow, he didn't think the old revolutionary would have raged too much at his death. Rosa was dead, and Emil had never expected to live long, never really hoped to live to see the triumph of his Cause. Only final victory was important, not his personal part in it, and as revolutionaries went, Emil Brunner had beaten the odds by a lot of years from Spain and before, through the Stalin days and Joe McCarthy, to J. Edgar Hoover and Viet Nam.

Jackson sat down facing the dead man, took out one of his Mexican cigars. He put it back. A piece of paper lay just under the couch, just out of the pool of drying blood. He bent and picked it up. It was a check, uncanceled. A dividend check from Bache & Co. made out to Amanda Blake on behalf of Monsanto Chemical Company. Jackson turned it over. Amanda Blake had endorsed it. So had Frank Walton. The ex-Marine's endorsement was the last.

Walton could have given the endorsed check to Emil Brunner. It could have fallen from Brunner's pocket. Or Walton could have carried it here himself. But Frank Walton was still in jail. Or was he? Amanda Blake had said so. Then, Frank Walton could have given the check to someone else. The endorsement meant that Walton had probably intended to cash it where he was known, and for some reason had . . .

Thinking too hard, Jackson heard the car coming down the steep drive only when it had almost reached the front of the cabin. He glided quickly to the front window, his little Mauser out in his hand. The car was an old Chevy sedan, one he had seen somewhere before. He knew when the driver got out and stood looking expectantly at the cabin—Frieda Brunner. The wife of the dead man called out in the late sunlight:

"Emil? Emil? Where are you?"

The wife stood there with her worn face narrowing to a kind of anger. Her flat eyes watched the cabin door, the harsh downward lines of her once-pretty face deepened in the sun like the cuts of a steel etching.

"Don't you even come to meet me anymore!" Frieda Brunner called out, angry.

The man on the couch didn't hear the voice or the anger. Jackson went to the front door, stepped out into the shadows of the low porch. Frieda Brunner walked toward him, still angry, and then stopped and peered at him. She couldn't quite see him in the shadows.

"Mrs. Brunner, don't—" Jackson began.

"Oh," Frieda Brunner said, "it's you again. Jackson, isn't it? Emil didn't say you'd be here. He called, told me to meet him . . . He is here, isn't he? If he's gone again, I'll—!"

"He's here, Mrs. Brunner," Jackson said. "He—"

But the woman was already past him and going in the front door of the cabin. Jackson didn't stop her. He went in behind her. She had stopped halfway across the room. She saw Emil on the couch. Then she looked away and all around the bare room. She looked at the wide picture window and out at the view. Then, slowly but firmly, she looked back at the couch and the blood on the floor and the dead man.

"So?" she said.

She looked around again. She saw the one wooden armchair in the room. She stepped to it, sat down. For some time while Jackson didn't speak or move, Frieda Brunner sat and looked at the body of her husband. Her face was quiet, stiff. Then she sat back and closed her eyes. There were no tears. She made no sound at all beyond her slow breathing.

"Mrs. Brunner?" Jackson said. "Are you all right?"

She remained unmoving, her eyes closed, for some few more seconds, as if whatever was in her mind now formed a barrier to outside words, slowed them down in their passage to her brain. Then she sighed. A deep, slow sigh like a valve releasing. She opened her eyes, looked at the dead man once more. Then she opened her handbag, took out a cigarette, lit it, and leaned forward in her chair.

"He'd already fought ten years when I met him," she said. "In Germany first, then Spain. France, too, and Russia for training. Then he came here. After that we went everywhere, across the world—to fight, destroy, tear down so that others could come after us and build the better world. Then Rosa came. After that it wasn't the same. I was alone a lot. I didn't mind. Emil changed. No, I changed. His life was always the Cause, only the Cause—mindless, a walking act of terrorism, anything that hurt the Establishment no matter how small or useless in the end. Now he's dead. He had to be dead this way, someday. He knew it. They all lead to only that, the causes. Rosa's dead, and now he's dead."

She seemed to think about it all for a time as she smoked. "You live with a man most of your life, and you really live with him so little. You live with yourself. So many years to feel so little. Is it us, people like Emil and me, or is it every man and woman? For Rosa I'll cry a long time. I don't feel any tears for Emil. We lived almost everywhere, but we really lived nowhere. Inside our separate skins."

"You say he called you to come here?" Jackson said.

"Yes," she said. She looked at Jackson. "Why?"

"He had some plan. For the movement. Do you know what?"

"No. I haven't seen him since the day before the explosion where Rosa . . . Why kill him, Jackson?"

"You're sure he didn't tell you anything when he called you to come here?"

"No. He didn't tell me much about what he was doing the last years. Anyone before me. If he didn't tell you, he told no one. You don't have to worry."

"You can't tell me anything about who might have killed him and why?"

She blinked up at him. "Who? Why?" She crushed out her cigarette, shook her head. "You don't have to be scared of me. I don't know why you killed Emil, and I don't care. He's dead. The movement has its reasons, I was trained to that. You found him, and you killed him. If I know Emil, he probably tried to kill you. I understand. Don't worry about—"

Jackson snapped, "I didn't kill him, Mrs. Brunner!"

He saw her looking at his hand, realized that he was still holding his little Mauser. She looked at the blood still red on the floor. Her face went vacant, empty.

"It doesn't matter," she said. "Nothing matters, we all die sooner or later. Maybe you did him a favor."

"Mrs. Brunner, he was dead when—"

But he sensed that she was gone, transported inside to some other world of her own. Jackson had to decide what . . .

He heard the cars stop on the drive above. Three cars that came up fast. Jackson jumped to the front window again. He couldn't see the cars on Mountain Drive, but he saw the three men in Sheriff's Office uniforms walking warily down the steep driveway, their pistols out.

Coincidence? No. Someone had called them!

He turned to talk to Frieda Brunner. She was gone.

The door was open. Jackson heard no car start, turned back to the window just as the dead man's wife appeared outside walking up the steep driveway toward the slowly advancing police. Her face was vague, ravaged, and Jackson sensed that she had heard nothing that he had said. She had come in, found Emil dead, and found Jackson with a gun in his hand. She could see it only one way—he had been looking for Emil—and she would tell it that way.

His gun wasn't the murder weapon, he knew that. The police out there didn't know that, and they might not wait. But that wasn't the real danger.

Even if they waited to be sure he was the killer, they would have to arrest him. They would find his equipment case in the rented car. Frieda Brunner would tell them that he was a Weatherman. So would others, his cover was good. To prove he wasn't he would have to send them to Sergeant Prather in Gilmore. His whole involvement would come out, and that wouldn't clear him, no.

To clear himself he would have to reveal his whole career, end it.

Even that wasn't the worst—in jail, clearing himself, he wouldn't find the killer of Emil Brunner. Or of Rosa. By the time he cleared himself and they listened to him, the whole case could have slipped to Cuba.

Jackson thought all this while Frieda Brunner was walking halfway up the drive toward the waiting police.

He crossed the bare room into the kitchen, climbed out a kitchen window, and slipped off into the trees and heavy brush.

Once out of sight, he began to run.

Part Three

16

Jackson ran all that night.

He walked through the dark city and the hills, but inside he was running all the way. On the run.

He needed a car. He needed equipment.

At 10 P.M. he stood in the shadows across from his office suite in the landscaped office building. A police car waited in the shadows. They were after him.

At 11 P.M. he circled the isolated Montecito garage of Lou Onager. Onager was an ex-paratrooper Jackson had once worked with behind the lines in Korea. There were no police cars around the garage. Jackson softly whistled a precise pattern that imitated a mockingbird in the night— but not quite a normal mockingbird sound. If Lou Onager was listening, he would recognize the signal. And if the police had been there, Onager would be listening.

Jackson repeated the signal three times. From inside the garage, a man began to beat on a tire rim—an exact rhythm of beats. The police had been there, and the noise told Jackson that they still were. The police were hidden inside the garage, waiting, and Lou Onager couldn't help him tonight.

He walked off again into the darkness.

If they had learned of his close connection to Lou Onager, they had learned a lot about him already. Too much. They would be at his house, but it was a chance he would take.

With luck, he could outwait them up there.

It was past midnight when Jackson finally worked his way across the countryside, and up the side of his mountain to the *barranca* just below his glass-and-redwood house on its perch. He crouched in the thick mesquite. Kate Chapman's small Mercedes was parked in his garage. There was no other car, but Jackson made no move to leave the cover of the *barranca*.

He could see Kate moving around inside. He saw no one else, but he didn't have to. Kate knew he would be out in the night at some time, coming for his spare equipment if nothing else, and she was playing her role. Only she moved in the house, but her face and shoulders when he could see them, and her shadow on the drapes when he couldn't, made it clear that she was talking to someone!

A policeman was inside. The problem was how to get him out where Jackson could handle him. How to get to the house and his equipment without involving Kate Chapman later.

He was thinking of how to lure the policeman out, when a car stopped far down on Coyote Road below. It had stopped at the entrance to his private road. There were no other houses on his road. Jackson melted closer to the ground, his eyes fixed on where his private road first came out of the trees. He swore to himself that his infrared scope was in his equipment bag.

The night became too silent. The birds quieted, and the small animals in the brush were still. Jackson heard nothing, only the animals and birds did. Someone was moving in the night up the road toward his house. Someone who didn't want to be seen or heard. Not the police. A silent approach, expert, and Jackson heard nothing until a rock rattled to the far left not ten yards from where he crouched in the *barranca*.

A face appeared rising up from the ground in the light from the house. Then shoulders, and the whole man gliding across the open yard to a tall eucalyptus between the *barranca* and the house. Jackson knew the tall shape, and the face.

Frank Walton.

The big ex-Marine watched the house for some time. Then he crouched down lower. Jackson guessed that Walton had just realized that Kate Chapman wasn't alone in the house. Bent low, Walton limped close to the house, moved under the windows, and peered inside. Jackson saw his chance.

He drew his small Mauser, and while Frank Walton was still peering in the window, Jackson fired a single shot into the night.

Frank Walton jumped up at the window as if he'd been shot at, turned, and limped across the open yard toward the road. A reflex action, a kind of panic, and inside the house the policeman on stakeout made the same mistake. Jackson had counted on that.

The door of his house flung open, and a short, broad man in a brown suit came out with a gun in his hand. The man saw Frank Walton just as the ex-Marine reached the road and began to disappear.

"Halt! Stop!" the man in the brown suit shouted.

He came running out, fired a warning shot into the air.

"Jackson! Stop!"

The man ran on after Walton.

Jackson slipped out of the *barranca*, along the edge of the brush to where the short man would pass. He was there when the policeman came racing up, went past, and Jackson hit him once on the back of the head with his little

Mauser. The detective skidded on his face and banged into a tree. He lay still.

Jackson took his gun, found his handcuffs, handcuffed his hands behind his back, gagged him with a piece of his shirt, picked him up, and carried him back to the house.

Kate Chapman met him at the door. Neither big nor small, her height and weight in perfect proportion. Her oval face had a dark complexion like smooth, olive-colored marble. Her hair was dark and long, her body curved full under a short green dress. Her face was serious as she saw Jackson carrying the detective over his shoulder, but he saw something like excitement in her large, dark eyes. Almost a wild pleasure.

"Is he—?" Kate said.

"Knocked out," Jackson said, smiled. "All detectives have hard heads. Bring me some rope from my workshop."

He carried the detective through the large, brightly colored living room, through his bar and poker room, through his bedroom with its big bed and library, into a rear storage room. The stocky detective was beginning to come out of it as he set him down on the floor. Jackson stepped out of the storage room as Kate Chapman came with the rope.

"No, stay out. He's waking up, I don't want him to see you. Make me a double Scotch and two sandwiches, roast beef."

He stepped back into the storage room. The detective was awake, glared at him over the gag. He didn't waste his energy on useless struggling—an experienced man. Jackson squatted down, tied the man's legs and hands together.

"I'm going to leave you here. They'll find you pretty soon. I didn't kill Brunner, he was dead when I got there, but you'd give me a hard time. I haven't got time. I'm going to deliver the killer. Don't count on Kate Chapman, she's tied outside, too."

The detective only glared. Jackson left him there with a light on. It would make the wait a little easier.

In the kitchen, Kate Chapman had his drink and sandwiches ready. He drank first. She sat on a high stool watching him, her own drink beside her on the serving counter. In the short green dress she was not making it any easier to run. Maybe she didn't want to make it easy.

"What do they know, Kate?" Jackson asked as he drank. The Scotch was calming him, easing the ache in his weariness.

"The Brunner woman told them she found you over her husband with a gun. She says you were looking for him, and you obviously found him. She admitted she knew no reason for you to kill him, but that you were both members of a Weatherman terrorist group. She knew you lived in Santa Barbara."

He nodded. "About what I thought. Who called them to come to the cabin?"

"They didn't tell me that."

"What do they think?"

"A Weatherman internal fight, a political killing."

"Swell," Jackson said. He began to eat. "To clear myself I'd have to tell everything, even with the Gilmore cops to talk for me. Even that might not do it now—I could have ditched the murder gun by now. Even if they believed me, my work would be over as Kane Jackson Associates. I'd have to start all over, if I could, and somewhere else. I like it here."

"So do I," Kate said. She was listening closely, but there was something distracted about her dark eyes, distant.

"I like the money Kane Jackson makes, a new name would make nothing for a long time."

"I like the money you make," Kate said.

"So now I really better go out and find out what the hell has been happening. To hell with justice, retribution, or the safety of society. The real incentive—self-interest."

"Maybe it's all they've left us," Kate said.

Jackson finished his first sandwich. While he ate the other, Kate made him another double Scotch. She perched back on her stool in the short dress.

"The man that detective went after was Frank Walton. He's out on bail, or a writ. The question is how long? What did he want here? He could have tumbled to what I did to him, he's not a fool. Or he could have wanted to know why I killed Emil Brunner, what I knew. Whatever, it means I have to move fast and carefully."

"I hope so," Kate said.

"Was anyone else around? Anyone call me?"

"No, Kane."

"Damn it, they're making me work for nothing! Play the detective without pay. Do you have to sit on that stool!"

"Yes," Kate said, that distant look in her dark eyes.

"That's teasing, Kate."

"Yes, but not if I plan to find a bed."

"Not if it's my bed."

"Do you have time? An hour at least?" She wasn't smiling. "I've missed you as if it had been a year. The danger, maybe."

"When we don't have time for that, we're as bad as all the fanatics I've got in this mess. What's the good of any of it, if you don't have time for that?"

"No good," Kate said. "Start now."

From the kitchen stool he carried her into the living room. She was beautiful in the light.

The bedroom was darker.

At some point, her full breasts soft against him, he heard the stocky detective kicking against a wall in the locked storage room.

He was half asleep when a car passed on Mountain Drive below and jerked him awake. It went on, but he sat up. The clock read 2 A.M. She stirred beside him, kissed his arm, clung tight. He picked her up close against him for a time.

"You have to go," she said.

"I'm going to tie you up. Get dressed, we don't want to excite them too much, or give them the right idea. They won't believe you that I forced my way in, but they won't be able to prove I didn't."

"Don't take too long."

"If I do, I'm finished anyway."

She smoked while he dressed in the same old fatigues. While he picked up his extra equipment case, she dressed. He came back and tied her on the bed.

"You might as well sleep," he said. "I'll take the Mercedes, they're looking for Kane Jackson anyway. Your Mercedes, say I stole it."

"I wish I could go with you," she said. Her voice was fierce, almost eager.

"Maybe sometime."

He kissed her lightly. She closed her eyes. He went out with his case to her small Mercedes. She was a woman a lot different from Cassie, his ex-wife who couldn't stand a spy in her life. Maybe she was the right woman, Kate.

As he drove down the private road he began to swear at Sergeant Prather, the Weathermen, and everyone else. Now he had to find who killed Rosa Brunner, and Emil. He had no choice. That was probably what Sergeant Prather and his bosses had counted on.

17

The Channel Marina sat isolated by itself on the barren expanse of dunes and coast that was Oxnard Shores.

Jackson had stopped in Ventura to take two hours' sleep in a motel, and now it was just past dawn as he parked for a moment on the road leading to the distant, isolated marina. A state beach was up the main shore road, and the Mandalay Station of Southern California Edison stood massive and smoking on the shore in the gray light.

Jackson studied the marina through field glasses. The boats bobbed in their slips with no sign of life. There was nothing among the windswept dunes and coarse grass. All the roads were empty. No danger, no police, seemed to hover in the bleak landscape. Only the bare frames of a new tract being built far off at the edge of the water gave any hint of life—some insect-like men already at work. Jackson studied them through his glasses, they would be good indicators of any hidden police. They seemed to be totally intent on themselves.

He started up again, and drove down the empty road to the marina. There was an air of abandonment to the place at the early hour. The main building was a two-story frame house, with the second floor smaller and set back. There were two smaller outbuildings—a store and a boathouse—and two long docks with some ten slips each. The boats creaked and grated in the slips. Jackson studied each boat.

All seemed locked and deserted. He parked out of sight between the main house and the store building, and went to the main house.

The lower floor of the house was a plainly furnished living room, a dining room, and a kitchen. Jackson went through them all. A narrow flight of wooden stairs led up to the second floor. Jackson started up the stairs. Adam Marker appeared at the top of the stairs.

"You're still with the group, Jackson?"

Jackson stopped some ten steps below the slim youth.

"Is there a group?" he said.

"Yes," Adam Marker said. "One setback can't stop us. You didn't come here to meet? Walton didn't call you?"

"Emil Brunner sent me," Jackson said, watched the youth. "Everyone's here?"

"They're coming. I'm first."

"Rosa Brunner's not coming."

Adam Marker came down the stairs. He went past Jackson, went to a window in the big living room where he could see both roads that led to the marina. Jackson followed Marker into the room. The small youth's thin face was still pale, bloodless, but he had changed since the night in Gerhard Myers' cottage in Los Angeles. He didn't shake now, the suffering was gone from his eyes, the line of his jaw was hardened.

"There's always risk, I've realized that, thought about it," Adam Marker said. "Accidents happen, some die, but we all go on. There'll be mistakes. We can't be concerned with our individual safety. It's not important that any of us personally see the successful end, just to work for it."

"So no more tears for Rosa Brunner?"

"No."

"No need to know who murdered her?"

"If she was murdered, it wasn't by us."

"Who then?"

"Someone else. The police. Our enemies."

"Do you really believe that?"

Adam Marker turned from the window. He studied Jackson's face, his whole big frame, as if he was trying to find something special. As if he thought he might see something on Jackson's tanned face.

"You want to think it was one of us, why? You were supposed to leave the group, go to other work, but you're still around. Why are you so sure one of us killed Rosa?"

"It figures, Adam."

"Me?"

"I'd say you liked her a lot, but she liked Frank Walton."

"Amanda is Frank's woman."

"For now, or maybe that's in the past. Anyway, jealousy can do funny things."

"No, I didn't kill Rosa. None of us did."

"It could have been political, not personal."

"She wasn't a spy, or an informer, or on drugs."

"Maybe one of you is really against Weatherman. Emil was an older revolutionary. You're a pacifist."

Adam Marker watched him. "When did Emil send you here?"

"Last night."

The youth nodded, seemed to relax just a little. He went back to his window, watched the two deserted roads in the brightening dawn.

"You're wrong about Rosa, you know? We didn't kill her. Maybe she wasn't murdered at all, your information is wrong, some freak of the explosion making it look like murder. It was just an accident. But we'll keep on. This is a technological society, it's vulnerable to any attack from inside, to sabotage. It needs people like us, the young, for its clerks and technicians. It has to use us, take a chance, never knowing if we're enemies or friends, and its delicate, complicated operations so exposed."

"But you need money, right?" Jackson said. "That's a key in this country even for revolution. What is Emil Brunner's scheme, Adam?"

"He hasn't told us yet. Do you know?"

"No," Jackson said. "When did you see him last?"

He tried to make the question casual, unimportant. A try, without too much hope. No hope at all. Adam Marker wasn't a fool, no. The youth realized that Jackson had claimed to have been sent to the marina by Emil Brunner.

"When did he say I saw him last?" Adam Marker said.

"He didn't say," Jackson said. He reached into his pocket, held up the small silver medal he had found on the porch of the cabin where Emil Brunner had died. "Is this yours, Adam?"

The youth looked at the medal. "Maybe."

"It has your name on it."

"Then it must be mine. Where did you find it?"

"Don't you know?"

"No, I don't know. Tell me."

"In a cabin on Mountain Drive in Santa Barbara. Where I met Emil Brunner," Jackson said.

Adam Marker was silent for a moment. He was looking at the medal in Jackson's hand. Nothing showed on his thin face that Jackson could see. But his mind was working.

"What's happened to Emil?" the youth said. "The way you're talking all around him. Dead? Murdered?"

"You said you saw him, Adam. When? Where?"

"Where?" Adam Marker's left hand jerked once. "Yes, it was in that cabin in Santa Barbara. We talked about meeting here. He told me he had a scheme working to raise money, but he didn't say what it was. I suppose I dropped my medal. He was okay when I left."

"What time was that, Adam? When you left Emil?"

"Time? Why, it was—"

The youth moved like a cat after food. Quick and sudden, running for the door before Jackson could react. Adam had the door open before Jackson was after him. It slowed the youth a few seconds, and Jackson made up five running steps. He was out through the door in time to see Marker go around the corner of the house and between the house and the store building.

Jackson went around the corner, and hit a sawhorse in his path at full run. He went over it half-sideways, his leg feeling broken from the impact, and landed hard on his left shoulder, skidding. All he saw were Adam Marker's legs before something hit him on the head, hit again . . .

Stunned, Jackson lay on the ground looking for a chance to grab Adam Marker's legs. He flopped over. His shoulder hurt and his left leg ached like flame. He couldn't see Adam Marker's legs anywhere. He couldn't see the sawhorse.

He couldn't see anything!

He was lying in the dark.

He sat up.

The ground wasn't ground, it was hard. He ran his hand over it—concrete. He wasn't tied, and it wasn't totally dark, no. Thin shafts of light from above and to his right. Very weak, pale light. Still early morning.

All right. He'd been knocked out for a short time. Dazed and unaware more than out, he had no headache. Unaware of being carried to where he was. All right, where was he?

He stood—and hit his head on a low, concrete ceiling.

Damn all!

He rubbed his head, bent over. Not too far, the ceiling about an even six feet high. His eyes growing accustomed to the dark, he saw cardboard boxes, wooden-slatted crates, and a low concrete room about fifteen feet square. A storeroom for the store building, yes. He went to the light.

It was a slanted double door, very heavy, with small spaces between the angled boards. All right, he was in a concrete storage cellar for the marina store. Now he knew where he was. Now he could think about getting out.

He pushed at the slanted double cellar door, tested. It didn't give at all. He pushed harder. It still didn't budge. It was heavy, but not that heavy, so it was locked. From the way it didn't give at all, it wasn't padlocked, or any kind of key-locked, it was locked with some heavy bar on the outside.

Jackson put his back against the slanted boards, braced his arms on the sides, doubled his legs up against one of the higher steps, and heaved upward with all his strength. The slanted door didn't budge. He increased the pressure until his legs were trembling like sticks, and then he sat down, breathed hard. Nothing. He took out one of his cigars, lit it, smoked, noted that he still had his Mauser. Adam Marker had just dropped him into the storage cellar and gone. Not carried, no, he was too big and Marker was too small. Dragged—unless Adam Marker had a lot more muscles than showed.

He had been in prisons before. He smoked. It had been a long time, but you don't forget. First you sit calmly. Then you try the most obvious way out. Then you inspect. He got up, and inspected. It was a good prison—four concrete walls, a concrete floor, and a concrete ceiling. No windows. A box with one exit he couldn't budge.

He had been in prisons. Alone. You make a plan. It doesn't matter if the plan has any hope, you make it anyway. To keep the mind alive. There must be something to think about. The illusion of hope.

There is always a weak point in what man builds.

Then, this wasn't, after all, a prison. A cellar, and above there was a marina. People would come. A few shouts . . .

No, people wouldn't come. The marina had to be closed, or the Weathermen wouldn't have picked it to meet. There were the boats, though. People would come to them.

Only he couldn't shout, not unless he was certain the people he heard weren't the police.

All right, but it wasn't a prison, and every cell had a weak point. He finished his cigar, the smoke hanging heavy in the small, low cellar, and inspected the slanted double door. There had to be hinges. There were—on the outside. That made it harder. But, again, this was a cellar not a prison.

He found a small crowbar used for opening the wooden crates, and two short, heavy, hooked knives for opening the cardboard boxes. He went to work on the heavy boards where the shadow of the hinges showed in the now-yellow morning sunlight.

Slow work. Jackson was patient.

The sun was high, he was two inches into the thick, seasoned board, when he heard people. Footsteps off toward the slips. He didn't shout. He stopped working and took out his Mauser in case it was the police and they knew where he was. In case it was Adam Marker back to finish him. There wasn't much doubt now who had killed Rosa and Emil Brunner.

A boat started up, faded away. Jackson swore. Not police or Weatherman. Just boaters. He could have shouted.

His watch told him it was just noon when he dug through

to the screws of the first hinge, broke the hinge loose with the small crowbar. The door budged when he put his back to it, but no more than a few inches. He went to work on the second hinge with the short, curved knife.

Another boat pulled away at 1:10 P.M. He had not shouted. He shouted when he heard the boat. No one came, his voice covered by the engine and the wind outside.

Fingers bleeding, the nails torn, he cut through to the second hinge just after 2 P.M. He used the crowbar to break the screws, put his back against the heavy doors, and heaved up with all his strength. The solid, massive door of two-by-fours raised slowly and the opposite side hinges bent. The door raised to vertical, and he was out.

No one was in sight.

He went into the main house. He searched each room, on both floors. No one. In the living room he looked out and saw his Mercedes still parked. Good. Where would Adam Marker go? No answer. He could wait for the others to come and ask. If they came. Adam could have warned them off. Was sure . . .

He saw that the telephone had been moved from near the door to a table beside a chair, its long cord trailing across the big living room. A magazine lay on the floor next to the table and the telephone. Jackson saw the telephone number scrawled across the magazine. He didn't recognize the number, it could have been jotted down at any time by anyone, but Jackson didn't remember the magazine being on the table, and the telephone had been moved. And he did recognize the number exchange—a Gilmore number. He dialed the area code and the number.

"Gilmore Athletic Club," a brisk voice said. "Hold on."

The voice went away. Jackson held. He didn't have to think too hard. The voice came back on, brisk and jovial:

"Yes, sir, now what I can I do for you?"

"Is Mr. John Marker there?"

"Mr. Marker? Sure is. Always in the afternoon. I'll get him for you."

Jackson waited. It was a long wait. A full five minutes that seemed like an hour. The voice wasn't so brisk this time.

"Sir? I'm sorry. He was here this morning, and I saw him come back at his regular time this afternoon, but we can't seem to locate him. I'm sure he's around somewhere, I'll try—"

"Never mind," Jackson said. "Thanks."

There might be someone else Adam Marker would call at the Gilmore Athletic Club when Adam was in trouble, but Jackson doubted it. He went to his car.

On the freeway he turned south and drove fast in the hot afternoon.

18

A moving van was parked in the dusk in the driveway of the run-down mansion in Gilmore where John Marker had his transient home. The door was open, Jackson walked in. Christina Marker saw him. She wore slim slacks and a dark red shirt and her face had a smudge of dirt that made Jackson's back stab. He thought about Kate Chapman. He walked to Christina Marker. Her eyes were tired—too tired to be just from moving.

"Where's Adam?" Jackson said.

"He has gone," she said.

The moving men walked past carrying pieces of the Italian furniture. Christina was packing boxes.

"Where to?" Jackson said.

"We move back to Los Angeles, a better house. Why do you pursue poor Adam so much?"

"Two reasons, both dead."

John Marker was in an inner doorway. In his shirtsleeves he looked tireder than his wife. He wiped at his face, came into the hall where Jackson stood.

"Who else is dead?"

"Emil Brunner."

"That girl's father?"

"Yes."

John Marker nodded. "Adam was here, he's gone again. Come inside."

They went into an empty library, the shelves without any books. John Marker sat in a worn leather armchair from some richer owner of the mansion. Jackson stood.

"He called me early today," John Marker said. "I was at my health club. He called the club. He said he had to see me. He arrived here about noon. He wanted money, a lot of money. He said he needed the money to leave the country. I told him he and his friends had used me, almost ruined me, and now he wanted me to pay for him to escape the justice that was coming to him! I asked him what kind of man he was."

The businessman's voice wasn't loud or angry. It was low and flat and mechanical. Like someone in a kind of shock.

"How much money?"

"Ten thousand dollars." John Marker looked up at Jackson. "He wanted ten thousand dollars. He said I had it because the insurance company had paid me. Ten thousand dollars when I barely have enough to get started again! When I really don't have enough to start again. I'll probably have to go back to work for someone else, and he—" The businessman trailed off. He seemed to shake his head to rid it of some weight. "Did he kill this Emil Brunner?"

Jackson held up the small silver medal. John Marker looked like a man hypnotized by the shiny object as it revolved in Jackson's hand.

Marker said, "I remember when he won it. I'd worked all summer to train him to sail the Star boat we had then. He came in second in the finals at our club. A father and son project, all the fathers worked that summer to train their sons. I remember how proud Adam was, how proud I was. We were happy then. He was a boy with the whole world ahead of him. We were solid, secure, maybe not rich."

"It has to be Adam's medal?"

"They gave the fathers the same medal. The mentors of the boys, you know?"

John Marker reached into his pocket, held up his key ring. The mate of the silver medal dangled from a short chain. It sparkled smoothly in the light, revolving like some distant beacon. In a way it was—a beacon not in space but in time. A beacon from the past when Adam Marker had been an eager boy.

"You think Adam killed them both, Jackson?" John Marker put his keys and the medal back into his pocket.

"I know he was there both times."

John Marker shook his head. "Why was he with those people at all? Why is he? Violence, terror, bombs! That's not Adam."

"It's not anyone's son or daughter, probably even Frank Walton's parents say that. But they do make bombs and use them. They've all lost faith in any other way to their better world. Almost when none of us were looking, and it's a short step from violent terrorism to murder."

"They put Adam in prison for refusing to kill, Jackson. I don't agree with him, a man fights for his country against anyone who wants to block it, but Adam went to prison rather than be part of an army that kills. Now you want to say a boy like that murdered two people?"

"When you stand outside your culture, outside its rules, pretty soon all the rules can seem unimportant."

"He wants change, but he hates violence and blood!"

"No, he doesn't want change. That's the mistake a lot of people make. He wants to destroy an evil world. He's beyond reform, lost to the main society whether it reforms or not. Nothing short of a clean slate and start over from scratch. He's in a different moral universe now."

The businessman moved his head, a helpless gesture. "I don't understand him, Jackson. I never will. I don't understand why he doesn't want what I want. I don't understand what is wrong with a man wanting all the good things for himself and his family. I'm a simple man, I want Christina, and a good life. I want to be happy, that's all. My share, you understand?"

"I do, but Adam won't."

Marker nodded. "He never talked to me. I never knew what he wanted or why. Especially why. I remember what a stubborn kid he was. When we told him to do something he didn't want to, he'd just stand there, sullen, and no punishment would make him do it. He always had this heavy conscience, so often depressed while his buddies were out joking, flirting." The father brushed at his eyes. Mystification in his eyes, and something else—stark confusion, maybe. "But he didn't murder anyone."

"He's a terrorist, a special kind—intense and emotional. Not like Emil Brunner. For Brunner violence was only a weapon in politics. Not like Frank Walton whose whole release is the violence. Violence against violence is Walton's measure of his own manhood. Not Adam. For Adam, violence is a kind of moral retribution on evildoers, a cry of exhausted idealism. When idealism is lost, retribution murder isn't so far away."

John Marker was silent. He didn't agree, but he didn't deny it, either. He sat as if he would never move, couldn't move. Invisibly fixed in the worn leather chair.

"I suppose he didn't say where he would go now?" Jackson said.

"No."

"Did you give him the money?"

"Yes. He's my son."

There was a world in the simple words. A complex world that could twist and turn but never end because a father and child never ended even with death, two tangled lives that would go on as long as even one lived. All of us, one way or another, doomed, or blessed, to the world of parent and child forever.

"Then he has the money to go anywhere," Jackson said.

"I had to give it to him, no matter what," John Marker said. "I had to help him, and I have to help myself. Maybe I'm wrong, but I have to follow my own road. What I have to have, my own business. The insurance money will help, I'll find the rest. I'll start again. Build. Build!"

There was a kind of violent fanaticism in the businessman's voice as strong in its way as the fanaticism of the Weathermen. An intensity that wouldn't be stopped, either. Jackson started for the door out of the bare library.

"If you hear from him, tell him he hasn't got a chance if he runs."

"I won't hear from him again," John Marker said. "Not this time."

Christina Marker wasn't in the hall as Jackson passed through. He heard her singing somewhere. A pleasant sound, a woman singing to herself as she went about work she liked.

Outside it was dark now. Jackson went to his car thinking about Adam Marker and ten thousand dollars. Money for escape? Why? The underground network was smooth, efficient and skillful. By now it was a well-traveled road to Cuba or Algiers, with the F.B.I. and C.I.A. just as glad, for the most part, to get rid of the militants. To the police, the whole group had effectively vanished from the moment they left the blasted chemical plant. Jackson had traced them only because he, too, was thought to be one of them, a fugitive.

At his car he leaned against it for a moment, lighting one of his cigars, and watched an elegantly dressed man come walking along the early night street. A bright orange sport jacket, yellow-brown slacks, an ascot at his throat under a pale yellow shirt. It was getting to be a peacock world for those not locked in some death struggle. Escape, and he smiled as the gaudy man passed his car. The man didn't pass. He stopped, approached Jackson.

"You're Kane Jackson, right?"

"Yes, do I—?"

A gun came up at him. "Get into your car."

The gaudy stranger held the pistol in both hands. His hands shook. His soft, weak face almost chalk white. Fear.

"Put that damned gun down," Jackson said. "You'll shoot—"

"No! Get into your car!"

Jackson got in behind the wheel. The stranger got into the back, closing the door and holding the pistol again in both hands as if he knew his nerve wasn't enough to hold a gun in one hand, or knew he had never shot a gun and didn't trust one hand. His voice was shaking now. "Drive to the Union Motel."

Jackson drove carefully down the dark street.

19

In a straight chair, Jackson faced the gaudy stranger who stood with his back to the motel room door. He was still pale, the gaudy man Jackson had never seen before, and he still held the pistol out in both hands, his arms rigid as if to bend his elbows would let the gun fall and take all his courage and resolve with it.

"You bastard," the gaudy man said, his voice shaking as much from fury now as from fear. "Ten years I worked to get where I was. Did you think of that? My whole life, wiped out in a minute by a jackal like you—for pay! A paid Judas. Is that how you always make your living, Jackson? On other people's blood?"

"Is there some other way?"

"No, maybe not, but you did it to me, and I'm—"

Jackson broke in. "It might help if I knew what the hell you were talking about. For a starter, maybe I should know who you are. I've never seen you before."

"Unger," the gaudy man said. "Kenneth Unger. Remember?"

"No, I don't remember. Fill me in." But there was something about the name. He had heard it somewhere. Where?

"You ruin so many innocent people to make your dirty money that you can't remember names? *Doctor* Kenneth Unger, does that help?"

Jackson made the connection, yes. "One of the two scientists I reported to Edgar Callison about. I remember now."

"Sure you do. A job well done, right?" Dr. Kenneth Unger said, the pistol jumping in his hands. "You bastard! What the hell business was it of yours?"

"How did you know I reported you to Callison?"

"How? He told me! The best in the business!"

"Callison *told* you?"

"Worried, Judas? Maybe he wants to bust you too! You told him I was planning to quit and work with John Marker, and he fired me the next day! Showed me my signed agreement with Marker, said Kane Jackson, best in the business, got it for him, did I think I could go against a man like him?"

"The damned fool," Jackson swore.

"Ten years slaving for Callison, building up *his* company for him, and he fires me without notice, without reference. I've got a wife, Jackson. A family."

"You should have thought of that," Jackson said coldly. "I ruined you, did I? The hell I did. You ruined yourself, Dr. Unger. Do you feel bad about what you'd planned to do to Edgar Callison and his company? No, you feel bad because you got caught. Play a cheat, you risk getting caught."

Jackson stood and walked toward the gaudy man. Dr. Unger tried to step back, but he was already against the door. He held the gun high in both hands, aimed at Jackson, but his hands shook. Jackson reached out, deliberately, and took the gun out of Dr. Unger's shaking hands. He looked at it, laughed.

"Safety not even off," he said, tossed the pistol onto the bed without even unloading it. "You couldn't shoot anyone, Dr. Unger, not you. Tricky dealing is your game."

The scientist suddenly stopped shaking, color coming back into his face, as if he was relieved to have the gun taken, his resolve removed. He pushed past Jackson, went to a chair, sat down. He lit a cigarette with steady hands, his voice stronger now that he was no longer pretending to be what he could never be. A man of words, Unger, not action.

"You're a tough man, Jackson, aren't you? Does that make you feel good? Do you enjoy your work? Destroying men you've never met, who've never done anything to you?"

Jackson shook his head. "Don't try to make me feel guilty about you, Dr. Unger. I don't. Not for you and your buddy. You played a cheating game, tried to make a good deal for yourselves by knifing Edgar Callison. All under the table and in the dark."

"It's a competitive world. A man looks out for himself."

"Nuts," Jackson snapped. "Fair competition, yes, but what you and your buddy planned wasn't fair competition. Go to Callison, lay it on the line, a better deal or you go with John Marker's new company. But not you. Maybe because you knew Marker had already swiped Callison's secrets. But mostly just because you didn't want any risk. Maybe John Marker's deal isn't good enough, then you stay with Callison. No risk. I don't feel guilty at all. You and your buddy got what you had coming."

Dr. Unger laughed bitterly. "My buddy? You mean the good Dr. Eliot Klein, the other traitor to Edgar Callison's empire? You don't know your world so well after all. You think Callison fired him too? Oh no, sir! Dr. Eliot Klein is too important, he's got too much in his head. Out of compassion, Callison forgave Dr. Klein. That's the way it works, you see? Dr. Klein is too valuable to be fired. All advantage, self-interest. You give me a big lecture about cheating, looking out only for myself. Where do you think I learned that? Tycoons like Edgar Callison, that's where. We're not people to him, just tools. He didn't need me, so the very righteous and indignant axe. But Eliot Klein? Oh no, all is forgiven. Just don't do it again, Eliot, okay?"

"He only fired you?"

"That's right. Does that make you feel a little bad?"

"Why is Dr. Klein so important to Callison?"

"Why?" Dr. Unger shrugged. "The adhesive process, of course. The new adhesive. Klein's got more of that in his head than even John Marker has. The work we did after Marker quit to go on his own."

"The new process and product John Marker took away with him? The research and process report he stole, was going to build his new company around?"

"Sure, why do you think Marker was going to hire us, pay a fat bonus? The adhesive process was all Marker really cared about, and all Callison cares about as far as Klein and I are concerned. Klein was smarter than I was, damn him. Without Klein, even Edgar Callison can't go ahead with the adhesive process and make it pay. So, bingo, Klein is forgiven."

"You mean," Jackson said, frowning thoughtfully, "that if Callison lost Dr. Klein, not only would John Marker have the new adhesive to sell, Callison *wouldn't* have had it? If he lost Klein and you, he would have been in trouble?"

"Trouble in spades. Callison's put a lot of time and money into the new adhesive. He—" Dr. Unger stopped, began to smile with a light dawning in his eyes. "You think maybe Callison had so much to lose if Johnny Marker got us, he blew up that plant just to be sure Marker couldn't use us? You know, Jackson, that's a nice thought. Yes, I like that."

"You have any idea where Edgar Callison was that night?"

"No, none," Unger said, smiled. "Do you, maybe?"

"Was there any way Callison could have been sure you two were jumping to John Marker before I reported to him?"

"We didn't tell him, but, then, who knows? He must have guessed or he wouldn't have hired you. I don't figure you come cheap. Maybe he just didn't figure he'd take a chance."

"Maybe he didn't," Jackson agreed. Where had the company president been that night while Jackson was getting the final evidence that John Marker had pirated his process and his people? Maybe he had decided not to wait.

Dr. Unger smiled again. "Only the joke is on Callison and you, you know? Callison could have saved his money, and you could have saved yourself the trouble."

"Joke?"

"Johnny Marker wasn't going to get us to go with him anyway!" Dr. Unger said, laughed aloud. "It was all finished, *kaput*, a month ago. Marker couldn't come up with the cash, the big bonus! He was going ahead without us at all. We weren't even going to jump to Marker after all, and you had to fink to Callison and get me fired, you son-of-a-bitch!"

"I won't lose any sleep over it, Unger," Jackson said. He walked to the door of the motel room. "Get a job, and don't try to be clever anymore, it's not your game. And throw that pistol into the Pacific, all you'll do is shoot off your foot."

20

Jackson found a public telephone and called Edgar Callison's office. There was no answer. He called the company president's special home number. No answer there. He drove onto the freeway and headed for Los Angeles.

He left the freeway in Beverly Hills, found Edgar Callison's home on a quiet, elegant drive in the Hills. A fine, big house in Spanish style set far back on manicured grounds. The only light was at the rear. A houseman answered Jackson's ring. Edgar Callison wasn't home, the houseman didn't know where he was, or when he would return.

In his car Jackson thought for a time, then drove back to the Ventura Freeway and went north. He got off at Oxnard, drove out toward the sea and Oxnard Shores.

There was light in the Channel Marina main house like a distant lightship among the deserted dunes. A car Jackson didn't recognize was parked between the main house and the store building.

Inside the house, Amanda Blake lay on a couch watching Jackson as he came in. Her black wig was gone, the tall girl back in her tailored jeans and blond hair. The baby played happily in a traveling basket in a far corner of the large room. Amanda Blake's eyes were not friendly.

"You're alone?" Jackson asked.

"For now. I'm surprised you came here, Jackson. You should be halfway to China by now. The arms of Mao, safe from the native fuzz. Why did you kill Emil?"

"I didn't. Is Frank Walton your man, Amanda? The baby's father?"

"I told you that was none of your business. It has no meaning, anyway. When we win, women will be just human beings, children communal, no need for monogamous fathers."

"Maybe, but right now it has a lot of meaning—if Walton was dumping you, chasing Rosa Brunner."

She studied him. "You've got to have simple explanations, don't you? I killed Rosa because I was jealous."

"Not you, Adam Marker. I think he killed them both. Rosa because she wanted Frank Walton, and Emil because he knew Adam had killed Rosa. Emil was pressuring Adam to get money out of his father, I'm sure of it."

She still studied him, like a biology student examining a specimen. "You don't believe that things like jealousy have no meaning to us, that all that is over? That if Frank wanted Rosa it would be okay with me, if I wanted another man it would be fine with Frank, if Rosa was making love to both Frank and Adam it would be okay to Adam?"

"What if Rosa *wouldn't* make love to Adam?"

Amanda Blake sat up, her full breasts moving heavily under the tailored shirt. "You're not one of us at all, are you, Jackson? You don't think as we do, no. What are you really? Just a paid hand? Out for yourself? A mercenary working with anyone who'll pay you? Is that it, a mercenary?"

"In a way, I suppose I am, yes. That's as good a name for me as anything—a mercenary. That means I've been around, seen a lot, and believe little, right? Revolutionists aren't so different, Amanda. They get jealous, they grab for themselves, too. And they have their own private aims.

Maybe it wasn't jealousy, maybe Adam Marker is still a pacifist and blew up the bomb factory to stop you all. Rosa saw him."

"And Emil saw him kill Rosa, blackmailed Adam? You think Adam's father would pay to save Adam? After the explosion?"

"I'm not sure. I'm sure your father would pay if it was you Emil had seen kill Rosa. You were right, Amanda, your father was there that night, he saw it all blow, maybe he saw you and Emil, too."

"Did I kill Emil, too?"

"You had the time, you knew he was in that cabin."

"It was you the police found there, not me."

"I had no reason to kill Emil Brunner."

"Neither did I, Jackson."

"Maybe your father did. To protect you, or himself, or his money, or any combination. He's a strong man."

"In his way, I suppose he is," the tall girl said, nodded. "But he wouldn't kill anyone, that's not how the Establishment works. He'd buy Emil off. Use his money, buy off anyone. Why kill someone when he could always buy them? My father has the real power, Jackson. Compared to him and his associates, the Mafia are children. You can't really escape my father unless you cut him out like a cancer. He's like a leech sucking your strength and freedom with privilege. In Bolivia he visited me with caviar and steaks and money, money! He bailed me out of jail, over and over. He tried to smother me with advantages while his friends spread their claws over Asia, over Cuba, over the Dominican! He sucks the blood out of rebellion until it can do nothing. Well, he'll learn that Weatherman can't be smothered, that we intend war all the way right at home!"

"Maybe he's already learned that," Jackson said.

She was silent for a moment. "If he has, then he would blow up a thousand bomb factories, kill a thousand Emil Brunners to maintain his grip on power."

"And you, Amanda? What would you do to maintain your grip on total war against the country? No compromise? If you felt that someone was a danger to your total fight?"

"I'm my father's daughter. He taught me how to defend my interests," Amanda Blake said. "But I had no reason."

"Then Adam Marker did."

"Tell him, he'll be here."

"I don't think so. He's running, Amanda."

The tall girl only shrugged to that. She looked toward her baby. The child was sleeping now. Amanda lay back down on the couch and seemed to go to sleep too.

Jackson sat in a heavy wooden armchair. He closed his eyes and dozed. He didn't think Adam Marker would return. Yet—where else would the youth go? Maybe Frank Walton would know if he arrived at the marina next. Walton didn't arrive next.

Jackson dozed for over an hour before the sound of the car stopping outside brought him out of his chair and to the window. He stepped quickly behind the outside door, drew his Mauser, and was waiting when Adam Marker walked into the house.

"Stand right there, Adam," Jackson said.

The youth turned. His face had changed again. Not the suffering of the first night when they had talked of Rosa Brunner in Gerhard Myers' cottage, and not the hard, cool conviction of earlier today here at the marina. Something else, a kind of withdrawn nothingness, a vacuum face, like a man in a prison cell for something he never knew was a crime, and who has nothing to do and nowhere to go.

"I'm sorry I had to hit you," Adam Marker said. He ignored Jackson's gun as if he didn't see it. He didn't seem to see Amanda Blake. He went to a straight chair at a long table, sat down.

"Why did you kill them, Adam?" Jackson said.

The youth shook his head. "I don't know who killed Rosa. I don't know who blew up that plant. No."

"You dropped your medal at Emil's cabin."

"I don't know who killed Emil," Adam said. That vacuum look in his eyes, vacant, watching the sky out through the bars of his cell, immobile. "I went to see him about three P.M. We talked about his plan, he didn't say what it was. Just money for the movement. I left him about four P.M. He was alive. A small cabin below Mountain Drive. There was a couch, Emil was sitting on it. Picture window." Adam stopped, looked straight ahead.

"Then why run when I showed you the medal, asked you about Emil and that cabin?"

"I knew you wouldn't believe me. I was confused. I wanted to go away. Anywhere. I needed money. I went to my father. He gave me the money. Emil was dead. I was going to run. Then I knew Emil was only one man, the group would go on. I came back. Frank Walton will decide what to do."

"You decided I would believe you now?"

"Yes."

If Jackson hadn't known the real symptoms better, he'd have thought Adam Marker was under drugs. The stiff manner, the sense of moving within a mist that weighed heavily, the feeling of immense silence around the youth, the robot-like words. But Jackson knew the symptoms, and Adam Marker wasn't drugged.

"Why would I believe you now and not earlier?"

"I was wrong earlier. Irrational. I loved Rosa, I would never have hurt her. I had no reason to shoot Emil if I hadn't hurt Rosa. We just talked."

"No one else was there? No one came while you were in that cabin? You saw no one when you left? At what time?"

"Four P.M. I saw no one. The cabin's hidden in a *barranca*, just the view of the mountains out that big window. I always like to look at mountains. You couldn't see anything from the cell they put me in down in Arizona. That was the worst part, nothing to see except blank sky from that cell."

The youth moved at the table, rested his small hands flat on the table, sat very straight. "They told me it was bad to kill, man mustn't kill. They told me love was the noblest act on earth, to love my brothers. They told me to love other men more than myself. They gave me ideals, so I believed them, acted on them, said no when they told me I had to kill. I believed what I was told we all believe, so they put me in jail. I did what we say we believe. That made me a criminal. What is true, then? What does justice mean in this world?"

"And maybe some murders aren't crimes, then?" Jackson said.

Adam Marker didn't answer. The youth was looking beyond Jackson. On the couch, Amanda Blake sat up and looked past Jackson too. He had made no mistake this time. He had been alert, ready. Not his error, no, Frank Walton's skill. The big ex-Marine had made a perfect approach from outside, had come into the room without the outside door even creaking. Walton had a big .45 automatic.

"It depends on the murder," Frank Walton said. "Put your pistol on the table in front of Adam, Jackson."

Jackson put his Mauser on the table. Adam Marker

seemed to back away, recoil from the little gun. Jackson watched the pacifist youth.

"Now," Frank Walton said, "why did you kill Emil Brunner?"

21

Jackson said, "I didn't kill Emil."

"Who did?"

"How long have you been out on bail?" Jackson said.

"A writ, I know the law," Frank Walton said. The big ex-Marine held his automatic like a man who's used a gun many times, easy and relaxed. "I'll hear the story."

Jackson told him how he had found Emil Brunner dead, how Frieda Brunner had come to the cabin, how she had assumed Jackson had killed her husband, how the wife had walked out to meet the police and tell them. "Someone must have called the police to come to the cabin. Maybe the killer himself."

"Why have you been tailing Emil, all of the group?"

"Because Rosa Brunner was murdered."

"How do you know that?"

"We have ways," Jackson said.

"You mean the organization?" Frank Walton said.

"Yes."

The ex-Marine was thoughtful. "So you're investigating Rosa's murder for the underground? I wonder, you know? All that equipment you carry around. The way you operate —a real smooth investigator. Trained. You know, I've thought a lot about how the cops got to me and Raymondo Peña that night. Who told them where we'd meet? No one knew, not even you, right?"

"No, you didn't tell me," Jackson said.

"Right, but they were there. Now how? You could have told, and they were waiting to tail me."

"Did you see anyone tailing you? It was late, the streets empty. I don't expect you'd miss a tail at a time like that."

Frank Walton nodded. "Yeh, I wouldn't. No, no one tailed me I saw, and I did some turns to be sure. Still—"

"Why don't we think about Rosa and Emil Brunner," Jackson said, seizing on Walton's hesitation to change the subject, get the cool ex-Marine's mind off him. "Someone killed them both. I think the one murder led to the other. I think Emil knew who had killed Rosa. He was first out of that plant when it blew. I think he was looking for the killer of Rosa."

"So who killed Rosa?" Walton said softly. He was in his element, a hard, narrow instrument of destruction.

"That's the key," Jackson said. "Who was in the chemical plant that night to rig that explosion? Just four of you."

"Five," Frank Walton said. "You were there long enough. I'm not so sure about you anymore."

"All right, I was there. Did anyone see me come back? Did any of you see anything that I could have used to trigger an explosion from my room? From anywhere outside?"

He looked at them all. Frank Walton shrugged. Amanda Blake leaned back on the couch. Adam Marker did nothing.

"No, you didn't," Jackson said. "But what about the three of you. Or four. Emil isn't eliminated from the explosion just because he's dead. And there could have been someone else in the plant. Tell me just what happened, just where you all were before it blew."

"I don't think we—" Frank Walton began.

Adam Marker interrupted, still straight in his chair at the table. "We were rehearsing the attack. I was out in the corridor. It blew somewhere behind the big lab. In the storeroom where we had dynamite."

"Did you see the others?"

"No, not for maybe ten minutes."

"Earlier?"

Adam Marker stared into space. "We were all around, moving around, working."

"Walton?" Jackson said.

"I told you where I was—in the small lab where you made the fuses. I hadn't seen any of the others for maybe ten minutes. Before that we were all moving around, yes."

"And you, Amanda?" Jackson said.

"I was on the far side of the building. I didn't see the others, either."

"Where was Emil?"

"His rehearsal station was in the big lab," Frank Walton said. "But he was moving around, bossing it all."

"You saw him? Just before the explosion?"

"We all did, I figure," Walton said.

The others said nothing. They were all watching each other now. Jackson smiled inside, he was getting them against each other. The movement forgotten for a moment, just three people wondering about two murders—except that maybe one of them didn't have to wonder.

"And Rosa?" Jackson said.

A silence. Then Frank Walton spoke:

"She was supposed to be in that back storeroom."

"Where it probably blew," Jackson said. "Only her body wasn't found there. Maybe she saw someone and tried to run, but she didn't make it."

Amanda Blake said, "Who do you think she saw?"

"That's the question, right?" Jackson said. "Adam, who could Rosa have seen in that back storeroom?"

Adam Marker didn't seem to hear at first. Then he spoke without looking at anyone. "I don't know."

Jackson said, "Earlier, while I was making the fuses, did anyone go up to the second floor? The office section?"

"No," Amanda Blake said.

"Not me," Frank Walton said.

Adam Marker didn't answer. Jackson knew the risk of the question, but he had to take it now. Maybe they would miss the implication. If he talked fast enough.

"Were all of you together all the time I was making the fuses in the small lab?"

"No," Frank Walton said. "None of us were. We all moved around a lot. It would depend on just when you mean, the exact time. Any of us could have gone upstairs, probably."

"All right," Jackson hurried on. "Let's get to Emil. Adam admits he was at the cabin, says he left Emil alive, not yet shot." Jackson stopped, frowned. He went on. "Amanda knew where Emil was, had the time. What about you, Walton?"

"I knew where Emil was, I got out of jail in time, sure," Frank Walton said. "Jackson, what were you doing up on the second floor of the chemical plant that night? You were supposed to be making fuses in the small lab."

It had been a risk. Frank Walton had not missed the implication. There it was. They were all watching him, a wary light developing in their eyes. Any explanation was as good as any other now.

"I went to the toilet," Jackson said. "Adam, you said you left that Mountain Drive cabin at four P.M., and Emil was still alive? You're sure of that?"

Frank Walton moved his big automatic. "Never mind that. You went to the second floor to go to the head? Jackson, the first floor head is right down the corridor from that small lab! Who the hell are you, really? Why were you with us in—"

It was a pane of glass in the left window that smashed. A big pistol poked through the break.

"Everybody lay the guns down. Now!" a voice said.

Jackson knew the voice too well by now. Frank Walton laid his gun on the table near Jackson's Mauser. Adam Marker drew back from both guns. Amanda Blake had stood up. Marty Klegg pushed the window up and climbed in, the big pistol steady in the tall, skinny giant's big hand. Klegg stood inside the room, grinning. It was a tigerish grin.

"Sure took you people a long time to tumble to Jackson. Not that I blame you, he's a slick number, real slick. I still don't have him all figured out myself, like what he was really doing at Marker Chemical, but I've got a hunch."

"What hunch?" Frank Walton snapped.

"You cool it, mister. I don't figure it's going to matter much to you where I'm going to take you. All of you, this is the end, *fini*, the nice little barred rooms for terrorists." Marty Klegg grinned again, looked at Jackson. "I guess I'm going to have to blow your cover all the way, Jackson. I'll get some kick out of that, too. Spying on John Marker, right? That was why you got in with these nuts. A little industrial espionage job, I've checked some into Marker's record. He used to work for a bigger company, left suddenly. I figure that's what you are, Jackson, right? An industrial spy."

"Spy?" Frank Walton said.

"Sure, using you people to get into that plant. It was a shut-down plant, hard to cover his actions. A good idea to use you. I figure he turned you in, too, Walton. Then after Rosa Brunner turned up murdered, I figure the cops put pressure on Jackson to go underground again and investigate. Yes, Jackson?"

"Turned me in?" Frank Walton said. "How, he didn't even know where I was going."

Klegg laughed. "Hell, you never heard of a homing signal? You took his car, I'll bet, and he had it rigged with a homer, or something like that. The cops followed the signal."

Frank Walton, the others, seemed to have forgotten all about Marty Klegg and his gun. They watched Jackson with both alarm and anger. Jackson could see any chance of finding the killer of the Brunners fading. If Klegg turned them all in, Jackson would get nothing more out of them. His own cover would be blown, but that wasn't it now, no. He needed some time, some help, to find a killer.

"All right," Jackson said. "I'm not a Weatherman, never was. I don't even think you're right or have a chance. I'm what Klegg says I am, yes. I did turn in Frank Walton, and I am working for the police. I'm looking for a killer—and I think I've found one. You understand? I think I know who killed the Brunners and why, but I've got to have some time, and some help. I'm not interested in turning any of you in anymore, the way Klegg there is. You can all run, you'll have to now anyway. I just want a killer."

They said nothing. Jackson looked at Marty Klegg.

"Turn us all in, Klegg, a killer gets away. I mean it. I've got to have some time—"

Marty Klegg looked at Jackson and laughed again. He was feeling pretty powerful. He waved his pistol at Jackson.

"Tell you what, Jackson. You come on with them and me, and you can tell the cops your story. They'll help you find your killer, right? Of course," he stepped closer to Jackson, waved the pistol more, grinned, "it'll bust your cover all to pieces, but that won't make me sad." He glared straight at Jackson. "No, I don't like being pushed around by some punk—"

Klegg glared his hate at Jackson, and Amanda Blake jumped. Klegg had moved too close, turned too far away, from the unarmed woman. She jumped and had his arm. She was strong, athletic, and she leaned all her strength on the skinny giant's arm. Klegg staggered a moment, then, his long arm moving like a whip, hurled her away from him, cursing her.

Jackson stepped toward the skinny detective. Klegg got his gun up, covered Jackson. Jackson stopped.

Klegg saw Frank Walton too late.

While Klegg had been throwing off Amanda Blake, Frank Walton had made his move. He had his automatic. He shot three times, slow and accurate.

The heavy bullets knocked Marty Klegg against the wall like a rag doll. All three bullets had hit. Klegg slid off the wall, limp, shapeless and dead.

Jackson didn't wait.

The kitchen door was close. He ran. In the kitchen one window was open. Jackson went through in a dive. His left shoulder hit the frame, turned him in the air, and he hit on his right side. Rolled, came up running.

In the dark he ran among the dunes. He stopped, circled right and back toward the house. He heard them out in the night. All three of them among the tough grass and sand, Frank Walton giving orders.

Jackson ran low and silent back to the house, around it to his car. He was in, started, and on the road out toward Oxnard before he saw the three shadows run up far behind.

22

In the early morning hours Edgar Callison's big, Spanish-style house in Beverly Hills was dark on its smooth grounds. Jackson parked in the drive, walked to the house. There was no sign of life, but the pale green Cadillac was in the garage. Jackson pounded on the outside door.

His knocking echoed in the silent night, coming back to him hollowly from inside the big house, and then there was the sound of a door far to the rear, and hurrying footsteps as Jackson continued to pound. The door flew open on the angry houseman in slippers and dressing gown.

"Are you insane? I'll call the police—"

"I am the police," Jackson said. "Get me Callison. Now!"

"You're not *our* police! In Beverly Hills our police are very difficult with strange—"

"Get them. Get the F.B.I. But get me Callison first! This is murder, you understand?"

The houseman didn't faze. "Mr. Callison is in bed. If you have business come back at a decent hour!"

Edgar Callison stood on the stairs in the dim entry hall behind the houseman. "What is it, Kelly?"

"I'm sorry, sir. Some maniac talking about murder. Says he is police, but he's certainly not a Beverly Hills—"

While the houseman had been talking, Edgar Callison had come down three more steps, now saw Jackson's face in the dim light. His big, pulpy face darkened, the shiny holes of his blue eyes in the dark narrowed.

"Jackson? What are you doing here? You're not supposed to come to me again!"

"You weren't suppose to mention my name to anyone!"

"I didn't! I never—"

"Dr. Kenneth Unger? Maybe Klein, too? The one you needed, didn't fire?"

The houseman had stepped away now. He watched his boss with different eyes. It was one thing to defend the portals like a lion, his job. It was another to defend when his boss obviously knew the stranger. He waited silently.

Callison nodded to him, "All right, Kelly, go back to bed. Jackson, come into the den."

The houseman bowed and walked away to the rear of the house. If there was any signal, any prearranged instructions in what Edgar Callison had said to the houseman, Jackson couldn't spot it. He followed Callison into a small, pleasant room full of World War II guns, mementos, model airplanes. An unfinished model of a P-51 stood on a large table surrounded by tools and debris.

"I like to work with my hands," Edgar Callison said.

The big, soft-faced man was in a black silk dressing gown flowered with giant Japanese designs. He didn't close the study door. He waved Jackson to a seat, but didn't sit down himself. Neither did Jackson. Callison looked away.

"I'm sorry about telling Unger. I was so angry, he tried to deny he was jumping to Marker. I had to tell him. It was a mistake. Did he—?"

"He came looking for me with a gun, Callison," Jackson said. "Lucky for me he hasn't got the guts. Was that the only mistake you made, Callison?"

The heavy man had begun to sweat again. "Mistake?"

"Dr. Unger said some interesting things. You want to

tell me now where you were the night the Marker Chemical plant blew?"

"On private business, I told you."

Callison found a handkerchief, mopped his face. Jackson took out one of his thin cigars, lit it while he listened to the house and looked all around. He saw and heard nothing.

"Dr. Unger told me you only fired him, not Dr. Klein. He said you didn't fire Klein because Klein was too important, knew too much about the new adhesive process—the one you hired me to find out if John Marker had stolen when he left you. That right?"

"Yes." Edgar Callison's voice was low now.

"In fact, according to Dr. Unger, Klein had so much vital data in his head that even you couldn't go on with the process without him. In other words, if Dr. Klein went to work for John Marker, it meant more than unfair competition, it meant you couldn't even compete at all—you had no process and no adhesive product."

"Well, yes, all right! Why should I have told you that? You charged enough as it was. If you knew how badly I'd be hurt, you might have tried to charge even more!" The big, heavy man dripped sweat now, mopped his face and hands. "What the devil difference does it make?"

"A lot of difference if you knew those two were going to go with Marker *before* I got the evidence from that vault. If you knew, you might have decided to stop John Marker before I got the evidence. Maybe with a bomb that night."

"I didn't."

"Maybe you thought you could get me, too, save yourself the extra money you owed me—and cover your interest in John Marker at the same time. I mean, if you blew up that plant, I was a big danger to you. Where were you that night?"

Edgar Callison licked at his nervous mouth. "All right, yes, I was near that plant—but I didn't do anything!"

Jackson let the admission stretch into a long silence. The big house seemed to listen in the quiet, safe Beverly Hills night. Jackson listened for any sound of someone near, of danger, but he heard none.

"Without Dr. Klein, you couldn't go ahead with the process, though? The research report wasn't complete?"

"It was complete up to when John Marker left me," Callison said reluctantly. "But the key to making it really worth while, Klein had in his head. He came up with the change after John Marker quit. Some other modifications, too. I had to keep Dr. Klein, yes, that's why I went to all the expense of hiring you, but I didn't blow up any plant!"

Jackson nodded slowly. "What did you do that night?"

"Nothing," the heavy company president said, almost with a certain bitterness. "I did nothing, I couldn't. I'm just not a violent man, damn me! He was out to ruin me, John Marker, and I didn't have the guts to stop him! I just stood in the dark, and watched."

"You were there when it blew up?"

"Yes," Callison said, shivered at the memory.

"Did you see anyone? Anyone at all—outside, or going in?"

"No, not going in. There were two men, sort of hanging around the way I was. A handsome man, very well dressed. He . . . he was familiar, somehow, but I don't know why."

"Do you know Robert Blake?"

"Blake? The industrialist? Well, yes, I've heard of him. Seen pictures. You think . . . ? Well, possibly. But why—"

"His daughter was one of those Weathermen."

"Robert Blake?" Callison shook his head in wonder.

"But I couldn't be sure, not even for myself. I never met the man."

"You said two men?"

"Two together. The other man I'd remember. Very tall, maybe seven feet, and skinny as a pole. Like a—"

Jackson broke in, "You saw them at the time of the explosion? Or maybe you saw them go into the plant? One or both?"

"No," Callison shook his head. "I saw them just standing in the shadows some time before it blew up. I didn't see them again. I couldn't say where they went."

"Think!"

"No, all I saw after the explosion was the five people who ran out of the plant. The terrorist group, I suppose."

"You mean four people. One alone, two together, and one last one limping."

"Two alone first," Callison said. "One just seconds after it blew up. Then a few minutes passed, and another one came out alone. Then a man and a woman, and the last one limping. After that I got out of there."

Jackson said, "That very first one, right after the explosion, can you describe him?"

"No," Callison said. "It was too dark. But it was a man, I'm sure of that."

"Yes," Jackson said, nodded. "So am I now."

23

The sun was above the railroad yards in Gilmore when Jackson drove up to the run-down mansion. Sergeant Prather and his two men parked behind Jackson. The four walked to the house through the weed-grown grounds. The swimming pool was smooth and blue without a ripple behind the house.

John Marker opened the door. He was in a dark business suit, his face calm, but his thick hair was only roughly combed, and his eyes were red and exhausted. He didn't seem surprised.

"John Marker," Sergeant Prather began, "I . . . ."

Jackson said, "Tell your men to look around for Adam Marker, Prather. He's here somewhere, we've been expected."

"No, Adam isn't—" John Marker began.

Adam Marker appeared in a doorway. "It's okay, Dad. Jackson's guessed I figured what he had in his mind."

"Where are Amanda Blake and Walton?" Jackson said.

"Who?" Adam Marker said.

Sergeant Prather said, "The Oxnard police found Marty Klegg's body where it was dumped. Frank Walton is wanted for murder now, Marker."

"I don't know a Frank Walton," Adam Marker said.

Sergeant Prather nodded to one of his men. The detective went and searched Adam, stood next to him. Adam wasn't armed.

"Where's your wife?" Jackson said to John Marker.

"Christina isn't here," John Marker said.

"No, she wouldn't be," Jackson said. "She's the reason, right? Only the best for the new, young wife. Everything for the perfect woman. The big daddy."

"What does that mean, Jackson?" John Marker said.

Jackson turned to Sergeant Prather. "You better read him his rights."

Prather said, "I've got a warrant for your arrest. I have to tell you—" and Prather recited an arrested man's rights.

"Wait for your lawyer, Dad," Adam Marker said.

"Good idea," Jackson said. "Prather's got enough to arrest you, Marker, but proving it to a jury is something else."

"Prove what, Jackson?" John Marker said. His voice was steady enough, but he held onto a table, his face waxen.

Jackson lit one of his thin Mexican cigars, sat down in an old armchair that had come with the house. Sergeant Prather sat down. The two other detectives remained standing with Adam Marker. John Marker hesitated, then slowly sat down facing Jackson and Sergeant Prather.

"You knew the Weatherman group was using your plant," Jackson said. "They were perfect fall-guys. Who would look for an insurance fire when a bomb factory was in the plant? You rigged the explosion and fire, killed Rosa Brunner because she discovered you, and later killed Emil Brunner because he'd seen you at the plant. You didn't mean to kill Rosa Brunner. You probably had the knife in your hand, she surprised you, and you struck out. You carried her downstairs. What kind of murder that is I'm not sure, it depends, but that's what happened."

John Marker looked around as if for help. He looked at

Adam, and then at Jackson. "Is it?"

Jackson nodded. "I heard someone in the plant early. That was you the first time, when you set up the bomb and incendiary materials on the second floor above the back storeroom. The firemen finally traced the start of the fire to there."

Sergeant Prather nodded. "Second floor rear, not the first floor. That's why the damage wasn't so bad. No locks, doors or windows forced open, so entry was by a key."

John Marker croaked, "Adam had a key. He let those fanatics into the plant. One of them blew it up!"

"Adam, yes," Jackson said. "He's what finally made me see it all. Adam and that medal I found at Emil Brunner's cabin. There were two medals. When I showed Adam the medal the first time, he knew it was *your* medal. You said once that he was your son, no matter what he'd done. Well, you're his father, no matter what you've done. So when I showed him the medal, and started asking questions about Emil Brunner, he hit me and ran to you, Marker. He hit me because he couldn't answer my questions about Brunner and the cabin—he'd never really been to the cabin. So he ran to you, got the real story from you, and gave you *his* medal to cover you."

Adam Marker said, "That's a lie, Jackson."

"No good, Adam," Jackson said. "The medal I found was all scratched as if carried for years on a key chain. Your father carried his medal on his key chain. But the medal he showed me was shiny, unscratched. It couldn't have been carried on any key chain, so it wasn't his. No, you gave him your medal to cover him, since I had his medal.

"When I met you last night you *did* know about Emil Brunner and the cabin. You knew the right times, and what the cabin looked like. But you made two mistakes. One, you said Emil Brunner had been *shot*. I never told you, you hadn't been near the police, you hadn't talked to anyone who could have known how Emil died—except your father. He told you about the cabin and Emil because *he* had been there. You said you saw the mountains out that big living room window at the cabin. You can't see the mountains from that window. It faces the ocean."

John Marker, said, croaked, "I was there, yes. Brunner called me, I went. But he was dead when I got there!"

"What time was that?"

"Four-thirty, maybe a quarter to five," John Marker said. "He was dead, shot, all that blood! I didn't—"

"Maybe he was," Jackson said, "but why were you there at all? Why did Emil Brunner call you?"

John Marker seemed to shrink in his chair. He licked at his mouth, but it was all dry. "I was at my health club the night my plant exploded. All night. You can check."

"Prather already is checking," Jackson said, "but I already know the answer. I called you there once. You're a regular. You go at regular times. If they see you come in, they assume you're there even if you're not. There are hundreds of members. When I called they said you were there —and took almost ten minutes to discover you weren't. It's less than a ten-minute drive from that club to your plant, Gilmore's a small city. You didn't want to be gone long, so you left the club twice that night. First to set it up, second to set it off. You timed the explosion to go off as soon as you'd walked out of the plant to keep the time down. We'll find no one actually saw you at the club during those two short periods. We may even get lucky and find someone who saw you leave or come back.

"Emil Brunner called you to that Santa Barbara cabin because he had seen you that night at the plant, was blackmailing you. Prather's already traced two calls from that cabin to your home number here. Emil charged them on a credit card."

Adam Marker said, "Emil called here for me, that's all."

"So?" Jackson said, nodded. "Well, it might work. You might just convince a jury with that. Funny, you're a total rebel, out to destroy your father's world, yet you'll try to help him. You know the truth, but you'll lie for him."

Adam Marker was silent for a time. The youth looked toward a sunny window and the blue pool outside. "He's my father. Nothing can change that. We're part of each other, I guess. Doomed to each other. I can break with him, his world, but not all the way. Call it a psychological limp."

"Yes," Jackson said. "I don't think you can help him, though. He had to buy his materials somewhere, Prather will find where. With what I've told you we know, and the obvious motive, it's a good case."

John Marker said, "What motive? Why would I blow my own plant up, ruin myself just when I was ready to go? There's your damned mistake!"

"Because you weren't ready to go," Jackson said. "That was the motive. You had the research data on the new adhesive you stole from Edgar Callison, the sales prospects, the cost figures. But to go ahead you had to hire Dr. Eliot Klein, and you didn't have the cash. Dr. Unger told it all. Without Klein you had no chance to go into production. When you couldn't pay Klein and Unger, your whole plant was a useless investment. You stood to lose all the money you'd put into it. You didn't burn up your plant to make a profit, just to prevent a loss. All the money you'd sunk in that plant was down the drain unless you could get it back. You did—by the insurance."

John Marker shook his head violently. "No! You hear?"

"Edgar Callison saw five people leave that plant that night," Jackson said. "A fifth man. He didn't recognize the man, but he proves there was a fifth person. With the rest, there just isn't anyone else who fits."

"Lies! Mistakes!" John Marker cried. "Those damned fanatics blew up my plant. That Walton! You—"

Sergeant Prather looked at Adam Marker. "Damn it, boy, he *used* you! He used you to rob the insurance, killed one of your friends. He could have killed you all. What kind of father is that? Tell us the truth, and I'll let you go."

Adam Marker was pale, drawn, but he said nothing.

"He won't turn in his father," Jackson said, "no matter how much he hates what his father stands for. His weakness, not ruthless enough. Still the pacifist underneath. Anyway, Adam *used* his father, too, didn't he? He took advantage, too."

Adam Marker said, "Are you any different, Jackson? Didn't you use us all for your own ends?"

"Yes, I used you," Jackson said, crushed out his cigar in an ashtray. "I wonder if that's all the choice we have, all of us? Who uses who? Use the other man before he uses you? Or some new world of faceless robots without any differences, any individuality, any private dreams and ways? Is it all the same, no matter what?"

He looked around, shrugged. "What was your poem, Marker? *Ah, take the Cash, and let the Credit go, Nor heed the rumble of a distant Drum.* You said Adam wouldn't listen to you, went his own way and would kill, or die, for a distant drum. I wonder if it isn't better than your way—to kill, and die, for Cash."

John Marker only glared hatred. "I didn't kill anyone.

You'll never convict me!"

"Maybe not," Jackson said. "That's up to the prosecutor and the jury. A good lawyer might get you off."

Sergeant Prather stood up. "We'll find out. Take them both, men."

The two detectives moved. One took John Marker's arm. The other took Adam Marker. They started for the door.

Jackson said, "What are you arresting Adam on, Prather?"

"What?" the sergeant said, stopped. "Why, making bombs! Terrorism. And he's a witness."

"He won't talk, and how do you prove the bombs now? John Marker won't talk, there's no proof Adam made bombs with that plant blown up. You've got no proof of terrorism."

"There's you, Jackson," Prather said.

Jackson shook his head. "I told you I don't want to be part of all this. I agreed to find your killer, I did. You don't need my testimony against John Marker, and I won't testify against Adam. You've got no case on Adam."

"Which side are you on, Jackson?" Sergeant Prather snapped.

"My own side," Jackson said. "A mercenary. Maybe it's all that makes any sense today."

Prather stood there for a full minute. He looked at Jackson, and he looked at Adam Marker, and he looked at his men, and then he swore.

"Leave the boy," Prather said, turned and walked out with his two men and John Marker.

Jackson waited until he heard the police car leave. Then he walked out alone. Adam Marker still stood in the big, old room of the mansion.

24

It turned out to be a long day.

Jackson hadn't slept beyond the brief doze at the Oxnard marina, hadn't eaten since a quick, early breakfast with Sergeant Prather. He was tired and hungry.

Adam Marker didn't come out of the run-down mansion until almost noon. The youth drove his old car into downtown Gilmore. Jackson was behind him. Adam met a man who had lawyer written all over him. They had lunch. Jackson got the chance to have a pair of hamburgers and a can of beer in his car.

Adam Marker delivered the lawyer type to the courthouse at 2 P.M. Jackson followed the youth back to the seedy mansion. At 2:30 P.M., Adam came out carrying one suitcase, drove off in his old car.

Jackson followed him to Frieda Brunner's tract house on Cortez Way. Adam was inside the house for fifteen minutes. When he came out, he got into his car, and at 3 P.M. was on the freeway heading west.

Jackson was still behind him.

In the late afternoon haze of Los Angeles, Adam Marker left the Santa Monica Freeway into Beverly Hills. Jackson followed the youth along the quiet, curving streets of the green and elegant section. Adam turned into the driveway of a smaller house, as Beverly Hills houses went, drove around the house and out of sight from the street.

Jackson passed slowly. The house had an empty air, the grounds needed work. Not an abandoned house, but more like one that had been rented out and was now waiting for a new tenant. Jackson had an idea whose house it was—the smaller house where John Marker had lived before he married Christina, the new wife. Jackson parked up the street, worked his way back under what cover he could find among the trees and hedges.

He moved around to the rear of the smaller house. Two cars were parked there. Jackson ran low to crouch behind one of the cars. Nothing happened. He raised up in the late sun.

"Walton! Amanda! It's Kane Jackson!"

For a few minutes, nothing happened. Then a window at the rear raised a few inches. Jackson saw nothing inside. But the voice that answered belonged to Frank Walton.

"What do you want, Jackson?"

"Some talk, that's all."

Silence.

"Listen, Walton," Jackson called. "I won't try to take you, I'll leave that to the police. Send Adam out. He can search me, see I'm not carrying a gun. Then I'll come in."

Silence.

"I'm no danger to you anymore, Walton. You've got no reason to kill me. I've told the police all I know already. They've got it all down on paper, they don't even need me. It's all out of my hands now. Send Adam out."

The back door opened, Adam Marker came walking out to the cars. There was anger in the youth's eyes, he realized he had been followed, but he said nothing. Jackson stood up. Adam searched him, nodded toward the corner of the house. Frank Walton came around into the open. The ex-Marine had his big automatic. Amanda Blake came out of the house in her tailored jeans and shirt.

"What do you want to talk about, Jackson?" Frank Walton said. "I've got nothing to lose now."

"You've got a lot to lose, you can still get to Cuba or Algiers, but I'm not here about you. I want to ask one question."

"What question?" Frank Walton said coldly.

The three revolutionaries all watched Jackson in the sun.

"Amanda there had a dividend check for Monsanto Chemical from Bache and Company. She endorsed it. Then you endorsed it, Walton. Who did *you* give it to?"

They were silent again. Then Amanda Blake spoke:

"That check, it came the day—"

Frank Walton nodded, "The day the plant blew up. I was going to deposit it. I didn't, we were too busy."

"Who did you give it to?" Jackson said again.

The three of them looked at each other.

Mrs. Frieda Brunner opened the door of the small, tract house on Cortez Way. Her ravaged face peered out into the night at Jackson.

"Mr. Jackson? Come in."

Jackson stepped into the dreary little living room. Mrs. Brunner smoothed her hair with a hand.

"I . . . I'm sorry I thought you had . . . They told me, the police here. About Emil, I mean."

"That John Marker killed him?"

"Yes," Frieda Brunner nodded. "For the insurance. The reasons men kill for. It's men like that we fought against all our lives, Emil and I. A good fight, a true cause, but—"

"Rosa?"

She nodded again. "I can't seem to care now. Go on, you know? What Cause matters? Rosa's dead. I just don't care about the future, any future."

"John Marker didn't mean to kill her, Mrs. Brunner. But he did. It happens that way. Nothing to do with the Cause."

"They never mean to do it, men like that."

"No," Jackson agreed. "Yes, he killed Rosa, Mrs. Brunner, but he didn't kill Emil."

Frieda Brunner nodded once more, agreeing, then looked up at Jackson, blinked, "What?"

"John Marker didn't kill Emil," Jackson said. "Emil was dead when Marker got to that cabin, just as he was when I got there."

Frieda Brunner searched her dress for a cigarette, found a package in a pocket, lit one. "Then who killed him?"

Jackson took the check from his pocket. "The last name on it is Frank Walton. Walton killed another man last night, he's on the run. I'm worried what he might do to cover his tracks. You know him too well. Do you have a gun?"

"Yes." She went to a side table, opened the drawer, took out a small pistol and showed it to Jackson. It was a pocket gun, .25 caliber. Jackson called over his shoulder:

"Walton."

The big ex-Marine came in through the door. Amanda Blake and Adam Marker were behind him. Frank Walton stepped closer to Frieda Brunner. The worn woman backed away, the pistol in her hand hanging down as if she'd forgotten she was holding it.

"I gave that check to you, Frieda," Frank Walton said. "The day the plant blew. Emil told me to give it to you."

Jackson reached out and took the little pistol from Frieda Brunner's hand. He examined it.

"Empty and dirty. She didn't even reload it. It should

check out," he said.

Frieda Brunner shook her head as if to clear a thickness from it. She sat down. She smoked. She put the cigarette out on a dirty saucer on the side table.

"Yes, all right," Frieda Brunner said. "He called, he had this plan to make money for the Cause. For the Cause! Money from Rosa's death! I went and I shot him. He gave her to me, my Rosa, and he took her away. His Cause took her. She was all I had for all the years. He took even her. He killed Rosa with his Cause, and I killed him. I don't care. It's all gone now, all the years and years. Gone."

She sat in the chair with both hands on the arms. Her face was gone too. There, but not there. Lost somewhere in all the years of the past. Somewhere with the only thing life had given her—Rosa.

Frank Walton watched her a moment, then looked at Jackson.

"Okay, you've got your killers. Now we'll go."

Amanda Blake and Adam Marker moved toward the door. Frank Walton joined them.

"Where to?" Jackson said.

"Anywhere," Frank Walton said. "They'll hound me for that Klegg, but we'll go on with the war. As long as we can."

Jackson said, "You too, Adam? Why, you don't hate the way they do. You tried to help your father."

"He's a product of it, this world," Adam Marker said. "A victim. They make us need the illusion of 'going' somewhere. A line from here to there: 'getting ahead.' But men don't 'go' anywhere except to death. We live in space, not time. If we understand that we'll end this 'success' society, build a human society. Success, wealth, power, they're all illusions to hide the fact of death. No, I want a different world, too."

Amanda Blake said, "If we have to make a desert of this world. If we have to explode it all and everyone in it!"

"You?" Jackson said. "I know you, Amanda. All you want is to be the hero of the revolution, all ego. Arrogant. You want to be on top. You want to deny everything that made you. But the only way you'll do it is by dying. Nothing less."

"Then that's what I'll do," the tall girl said. "But I'll take a lot of my fathers with me!"

Frank Walton said. "You won't stop us, Jackson. No one will."

"I don't want to stop you, no. You can't win, you don't even know what to fight. Your ideas of the future are stupid, childish. You don't have a future, so go ahead."

Adam Marker said, "We have a future, Mr. Jackson. It may take a hundred years, but it will come. It doesn't matter if any of us see it happen, it's just important to be part of it. I haven't been really depressed since I realized I was part of bringing a human world to life. Just Rosa, only a moment. We may not win, but while we try we're alive."

Jackson said no more to them. They went out into the night, Frank Walton last—the rearguard, the walking rage who would never trust anyone. They would get him for Marty Klegg, yes, but it wasn't going to be easy. It wasn't Jackson's problem. At a window he watched them get into their one car, and fade into the warm Gilmore night. Gone to fight on in their war.

Jackson helped Frieda Brunner from her chair, walked her out to his car. She didn't speak. He had her pistol in his pocket. He drove toward the Gilmore Police Headquarters, the pistol in his pocket would finally finish it.

He didn't feel good or bad. He felt alone. The John

Markers he knew. Men who had run the world ever since the landlords of ancient China who had taken half the crop of the peasants who worked their land while paying only one-thirtieth of that in taxes and then wondered why the peasants revolted.

The Weathermen he knew, too. People want final conclusions, the "truth" once and for all. People need to feel there is a design, a purpose, in the chaos of experience. So when today isn't good, they dream of a new beginning that will make it all right in one, simple act. A magical vision to escape the sense of being trapped by a purposeless history. A violent vision of truth that will give all the answers once and for all.

Between the two, maybe it was better to be alone. Maybe all a man could be was a mercenary living for today. For Kate Chapman waiting on his mountaintop.

He reached police headquarters, took Frieda Brunner inside.